HE FELT IT—
A PRIMITIVE, ANIMAL FEAR.

Mr. London turned and sa

The predator climbed

shift and dip. Its mouth o

sprang out.

Mr. London shrank back.

He was dead. Done for. The final dinner bell had rung—and *he* was the featured entrée.

But there had to be a way out of this. *Something.*

Suddenly, images of battles at sea exploded in Mr. London's mind. Swashbuckling adventures. He lifted the branch he'd been using as an oar and waved it around like a pirate's sword.

The Microvenator shrieked in fury and attacked!

PLEASE DON'T EAT
THE TEACHER!

by Scott Ciencin

illustrated by Mike Fredericks

Random House  New York

To my angel, my life, my every breath,
my beautiful and brilliant wife,
Denise.
Your spirit, daring, and courage are an inspiration.
I love you, sweetheart.
—S.C.

Text copyright © 2000 by Scott Ciencin
Interior illustrations copyright © 2000 by Mike Fredericks
Cover art copyright © 2000 by Adrian Chesterman

www.randomhouse.com/kids

Library of Congress Catalog Card Number: 99-67552
ISBN: 0-679-88846-2
RL: 5.5

Cover design by Georgia Morrissey
Interior design by Gretchen Schuler

Printed in the United States of America July 2000
10 9 8 7 6 5 4 3 2 1

Dear Reader,

Welcome to Book #4 of DINOVERSE!

Readers have asked me if the age of dinosaurs was anything like what I've written in my DINOVERSE books. According to the fossil record, it very likely was. How did the dinosaurs live? What did they eat? What about the weather and landscape? Those questions have crossed the minds of scientists. And the fossil record has given the answers to them, to me, and now to *you*.

If you've read the first three books in this series, you've already seen Bertram Phillips's weird science fair project in action. And you know that Bertram's M.I.N.D. Machine has struck again, this time trapping Bertram's science teacher, Mr. London, and three of his students in the bodies of dinosaurs 112 million years in the past.

To get back to their own time (and bodies), Patience McCray, Zane McInerney, and Mr. London must now find their way from prehistoric Texas to prehistoric Oklahoma, where fellow student Will Reilly is trapped in the body of a raptor. Then they must prevent an event that will change history from occurring. Trouble is, they have no idea *what* that event is! And Mr. London has just been separated from Zane and Patience through a ride on a nasty twister!

Can Bertram guide his friends through the perils of the Cretaceous and help them solve a revolutionary mystery? To find out, come back with me to a time when the world belonged not to humans, but to the most magnificent creatures the Earth has ever known.

Scott Ciencin

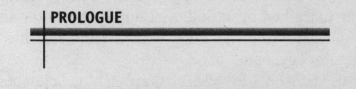

PROLOGUE

Wetherford, Montana
Mid-May, 12:25 p.m.
Four minutes after Time Displacement Event

Bertram Phillips crouched in a dark corner, his heart thundering, his face covered in sweat. Time was *literally* against him.

He was hiding in the basement of Wetherford Junior High, behind a wall of cardboard cartons. The floor was littered with gobs of chewing gum, splatters of sticky soda, and melted candy bars.

Bertram peeked around the stacked cartons. The lights in the basement had just flickered off. The only illumination came from a cocoon of crackling blue-white energies a half-dozen yards away.

At the center of that cocoon sat Bertram's creation, the M.I.N.D. Machine. It had started as his science fair project eight months earlier—but had quickly become something more.

The Memory INterpreter Device was ten feet tall and several feet wide. Over a dozen computer monitors lined its face. Thick cables and circuitry panels had been welded to its huge metal frame. A rectangular space had been hollowed out in its center and a chair sat within it, along with a table housing a computer keyboard.

Mr. London, Bertram's teacher, lay crumpled before the machine. Tendrils of energy snaked out from the rocking, shaking gadget and danced along Mr. London's body. Lightning sparked at his fingertips.

Bertram's heart sank at this sight.

Mr. London had told him the machine *was history*. The teacher had used those exact words.

Bertram had assumed that meant the machine had been dismantled. But, thinking about it now, Bertram realized his teacher hadn't lied to him.

Not *exactly*.

The M.I.N.D. Machine *was* history—history made real. It laid all of time open to its user, allowing one to visit any era, to see anything...

To *be anyone*.

No, Mr. London hadn't lied. But he *had* misled Bertram.

Why?

The machine was dangerous. It was far too powerful to be kept around. What happened when Mr.

London had reactivated it was proof of that.

And Mr. London wasn't the only one who had been affected by the machine's energies. Bertram looked down at his own hands and saw tiny bursts of muted light flowing through his fingers. He shuddered and hid his hands in his pockets, worried that the light might draw *their* attention.

They were the reason Bertram was hiding...

Because Bertram and Mr. London weren't alone in the basement. Far from it.

Shadowy forms rose up along the walls, snaked across the floor, and stole across the ceiling.

Hisses could be heard, along with the clicking of sharp claws, and the grinding of oversized teeth.

Tails dragged on the ground. Grunts and roars sounded.

Bertram shuddered. He was a baseball player, a weight lifter, and the smartest guy at Wetherford. Under normal circumstances, he could take care of himself. But what he was facing wasn't normal at all...

Bertram remembered the shock he'd felt when the crackling tendrils of energy first burst through the floor of his classroom. He recalled the stunned expressions of the students who'd been struck by that energy, their minds torn from their bodies and sent—

Elsewhere.

Bertram had seen a half-dozen students fall into comas as the lightning gripped them. He had stepped over the sleeping forms of a dozen more as he had raced from his class, across the hall, down the stairs, and finally here to the basement, where he'd sensed he would find the cause of the disturbance.

Just by touching the keyboard, Bertram had learned that Mr. London and three students had been sent back to the Texas and Oklahoma of 112 million years ago. Now they had to perform a mission—and prevent an earth-shattering event from occurring— or the world of here and now would cease to exist.

Unfortunately, Bertram had been unable to do more than connect briefly to the lost travelers. He was able to tell them exactly what had happened to them, and not much more. He didn't even know *what* the "event" was that they had to keep from happening.

All Bertram knew was that an amber key lay at the heart of the mystery.

Bertram had been able to tell them about the key, and then things started happening all around him in the basement. Many of the students who had been struck by the lightning, and had ended up unconscious on the landing, began to move. And to change.

The five teens on the stairs made sounds unlike any ever uttered by human beings. That became

Bertram's cue to get out of sight as quickly as possible.

He failed to get a good enough look at any of them to know exactly what they had become—or rather, what his machine had changed them into.

But Bertram did know they had been stalking around the basement, bumping into things, communicating in a language that seemed to be more than grunts and strange reverberating sounds.

If I could just get to the keyboard again, thought Bertram.

But the terrible *things* casting those frightening shadows and making those inhuman noises stood between him and his goal.

Suddenly, Bertram gasped. The five transformed teenagers rounded the corner where he'd been hiding.

They all stopped to stare at him.

"Wait," Bertram cried as they stalked forward.

He saw slavering, drooling maws and glowing crimson eyes. "Listen to me! I have to get to the machine, I know this can be undone, I can figure it out!"

With growls that might have been laughter, the five creatures who were once junior high school students leaped at Bertram!

Millions of
years ago

245 208 145 112 YOU ARE HERE

Triassic **Jurassic** **Cretaceous**

335 230 225 145 65 1.5

First
pterosaur

First
dinosaur

First
bird

End of
dinosaurs

First
man

PART ONE

CRETACEOUS

COURAGEOUS

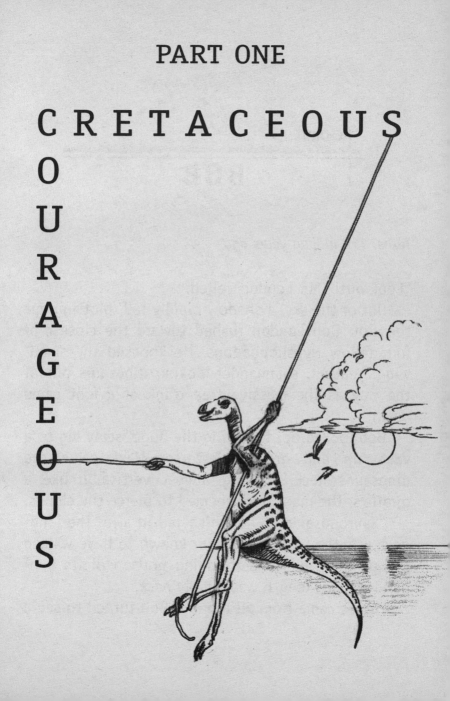

CHAPTER 1

BOB

Texas, 112 million years ago

"Look out!" Mr. London yelled.

Out of the sky, a shadow rapidly fell, blotting out the sun. Bob London rushed toward the closest of four fellow Hypsilophodons. He knocked the small, veggie-eating, salamander-looking dinosaurs out of the way as the massive tree trunk of a foot came down.

Bob looked up, following the huge, scaly leg to a vast hip and gray undertorso. Next came the dinosaur's neck. Angling almost vertically, like a giraffe's, the giant neck seemed to pierce the clouds.

"Sauroposeidon," he whispered in awe. The long-neck was the largest dinosaur known to have walked the planet. And an astounding portion of its one-hundred-foot length was simply *neck*.

Hisses came from all around. Bob turned to see a

pack of meat-eating Microvenators. They were surrounding the outer edges of the clearing.

The predators were cleverly blocking every possible avenue of escape. The only thing that had
stopped their attack was the huge sauropod that had
stepped into the clearing, nearly squashing some of
the prey.

Which includes me, realized Mr. London. Because,
although Bob London had spent years as a junior
high school science teacher, he knew now that
Bertram's M.I.N.D. Machine had dropped him into
another form entirely—*prey,* to be specific.

Mr. London studied the creatures who wanted to
eat him.

The Microvenators were small predators, not much
larger than his seven-foot-long, two-foot-high
Hypsilophodon form. But these dinosaurs had much
longer arms—arms that ended in three-clawed hands
that looked like talons! Their necks were long, their
heads birdlike, their eyes burning with hunger.

The Sauroposeidon began to take another step,
and Bob tried not to panic. The moment the long-
neck left this clearing, the meat-eaters would attack.

Then Bob realized something else. He was not just
any prey. He was *thinking* prey.

Moving fast, he snatched a shattered branch from
the ground and leaped high, driving it at the

Sauroposeidon's rising foot! He jabbed at the huge gray mass and fell back, branch still clutched in his little hands like a sword.

A rumbled cry of anger came from above, and the sauropod's leg smashed down into the clearing again.

The ground shook and Bob was thrown into the dirt, along with the four Hypsilophodons and the pack of predators.

He'd gotten the animal's attention, all right—and he'd gotten it *mad*.

Okey-dokey.

Just as two of the Microvenators charged into the clearing, the Sauroposeidon began to turn. He moved in a wide circle, his huge feet smashing trees and crashing down around the Hippies and their hunters.

"Come on and move!" Bob yelled, his words coming out as chittery squeals. "It's like playing Twister!"

He was a little scared, but excited, too. Since he'd come to this prehistoric world, he'd been an observer and never a participant. Spending that much time on the outside looking in had kept his emotions bottled up.

No more!

He zigzagged between the huge legs, helping the other Hypsilophodons, guiding them out of danger. With each strike of the Sauroposeidon's feet, the ground shook. The pack of meat-eaters retreated with shrill cries, unwilling to chance getting made into Micro-mush.

The predators scrambled into the woods. But they soon came back again.

Why wouldn't they just run away for good?

Suddenly, one bold predator came racing for him. Bob snatched up another branch.

The Microvenator's long fingers twitched and his maw opened wide. Bob jammed the branch in the Microvenator's mouth!

The surprised predator stumbled back, his sharp teeth stuck in the wood, his jaws forced open. Shaking his head, the predator ran back to his buddies, who gawked, then bobbed their heads, seemingly amused by their pal's attempts to dislodge the branch.

The Sauroposeidon was no longer stamping his massive feet, or moving in wide earthshaking circles. It looked like the immense long-neck was getting ready to move on.

The Microvenators sensed this, too. All chattered happily except the one writhing on the ground with the branch in its teeth.

Bob knew he had to get out of there. He watched the great sauropod foot rise, and an idea came to him. He leaped and managed to wrap his little arms around the sauropod's ankle.

He was going airborne!

Bob looked down at the quivering Hypsilophodons as the ring of Microvenators seemed to close in around them. The Hippies were smaller than him. Younger too. *Kinda like my students,* thought Bob London.

That's when he knew he couldn't leave them behind.

"Jump on!" Bob yelled. "You can do it!"

The others looked confused and scared. Riding the mammoth leg, Bob was lifted higher. In a moment, it would be too late!

Then the closest of the Hippies leaped up and caught a ride beside him. The other three ran for the Sauroposeidon's other foot and jumped onto it. They weighed so little that Bob was sure the giant dinosaur wouldn't even notice.

Below, he heard the angry cries of the Microvenators as they swarmed into the clearing just a little too late.

"Hah!" Bob yelled. "So much for you guys!" Then he craned his neck and saw where the sauropod's foot was heading.

"Heads down!" he called. "Trees!"

He hugged the Sauroposeidon's ankle and braced himself for the impact. When seconds passed and nothing happened, he opened his eyes again and looked down.

The Sauroposeidon had lifted his foot right over the clump of trees Bob was sure they'd crash into. The foot swung outward, making the lush greens, browns, and ambers below turn into a rushing blur. He felt the wind against his scales.

"Wheeeeeeee!" Bob yelled. "This is just like riding the Cyclone!"

He couldn't remember the last time he'd been to an amusement park, but he did recall one thing about roller coasters—no matter how high they rose, they always came down again!

Bob's stomach lurched as the massive foot he rode suddenly rushed toward another batch of trees.

"We'll have to jump for it!" Bob yelled.

The Hypsilophodon beside him squeaked in fright and didn't look at all ready to let go of the sauropod's leg.

But Bob yanked him free and they both fell toward a cluster of trees.

Gnarled branches reached up for him like old, brittle arms, but when he and the other Hippie struck, only a few twigs snapped. With relief, he realized their fall had been broken.

Then the Sauroposeidon's leg mashed against a nearby tree. The branch Bob and his buddy clung to shuddered like a guitar string, and he nearly slid off. He saw his new friend staring at him with wide eyes, but they both managed to hang on.

Bob thought of the rest of the Hippies. He looked past the vast drooping underbelly of the Sauroposeidon to the other front limb. It came crashing down, and the three Hypsilophodons slipped free just in time. They dropped into a tangle of leaves and branches as the huge leg battered down another tree and sent out more violent shock waves!

Bob waited until the Sauroposeidon had gone a good hundred yards before heading toward the trees, where the other Hippies had fallen. He raced along branches, making a wide circle around the smashed crater left by the sauropod. He found the trio of Hypsilophodons cowering together on a heavy branch.

"It's over," Bob said. "There's nothing to be afraid of."

He leaned down and started munching on some leaves. "See?"

The other Hippies looked at each other, then glanced downward.

Bob followed their gaze and saw the pack of Microvenators on the ground below staring up at them hungrily.

"Well, isn't that special," he muttered.

The predators began to scratch and scrape at the trunk of the tree. They hissed and snarled.

Above, the trio of Hippies clung together and shuddered. Bob and his copilot exchanged glances.

"We've got the high ground," Bob said. "Why don't we see where it leads?"

He didn't wait for an answer. Instead, he raced along the length of the branch and leaped to another hanging from a nearby tree.

The other Hippies scurried after him, while below, the Microvenators snapped and hissed angrily, matching their movements on the ground.

Bob ran from one tree to another. Sometimes he would stop and stand as high as he dared, hoping he might see some landmass—the top of a steep hillside perhaps—where he and the other Hippies could scramble to safety, but all he could make out was a carpet of green and brown leaves.

After a while, Bob felt ready to drop from exhaustion. The Microvenators chattered excitedly below, but he stopped anyway.

"Okay, I guess we'll just wait you guys out," Bob said.

The Microvenators began to dance. All except the one who'd gotten a branch jammed into his mouth.

He didn't dance. He only glared, some splinters still sticking out of his teeth.

Bob heard the Hippies behind him squeaking in fear as they looked at the predators below.

He knew he couldn't stay here. He had to return to the students who had traveled back in time with him—Patience McCray and Zane McInerney. He had to find "Ground Zero" with them and help Will Reilly stop whatever upheaval was about to occur in the time continuum.

Besides, there may have been plenty of greens up here, but there was no water.

Bob London tried to look at the problem the way he might have before he tampered with the M.I.N.D. Machine and brought himself and the others back to the age of dinosaurs.

Back then, he had been a teacher, a giver of knowledge. A rational man.

Now, ever since his brush with death on the great winds, he had felt like he was thirteen years old again! And somehow, not even the threat of these predators was enough to make him give up that feeling.

Of course, being thirteen meant being small.

And not too strong.

Bob shook his head. He had to be logical about this. He looked at the others.

"I wish you guys understood me," he said. "Maybe if we all went in different directions, the pack might pick just one of us to follow and the others could get away."

He was willing to be the decoy. But he was certain the Hippies would only follow him. He tried to think of some diversion, or some way of containing the Microvenators.

Then the sound came. A distant thunder. The leaves quivered and the branches shook.

He didn't have to see *them* coming to know what was happening.

"Run!" Bob hollered. "More Sauroposeidons! Run!"

He scampered off and the others followed.

Below, the Microvenators chased them.

But Bob and his friends didn't care. They ran as the footfalls grew louder and trees shattered in their wake. They leaped from one tree limb to another, the ground a shadowy blur beneath them.

Bob ran purely on instinct, feeling the strength of a certain branch, sensing the ones he should avoid, the ones that would snap beneath him and send him down to the predators.

The trees were becoming sparse now, the branches not reaching quite so far. He had to leap with all his strength to cover the gaps, and he worried that the others might not be able to keep up.

They were smaller. Like students. But they were also *determined,* and not one fell behind or skittered off a branch to disaster.

Bob made the longest leap yet, covering almost five feet, raced along a branch—

And stopped. He turned suddenly.

"Hold up!" he yelled. Then he saw the other Hippies charging forward, heads down. He looked over and saw that the gap between this tree and the next was at least ten feet.

There was no way any of them could make that jump.

And the thunder of the Sauroposeidons was growing louder.

"Look out!" he yelled at the top of his lungs.

The Hippies skidded to a stop just in time.

He looked around, hoping to find some of the vines he had spotted earlier.

Nothing.

Then the tree off to his left fell and a massive shape rose up before him, its head reaching for the sky.

Bob grabbed hold of the branch beneath him as a huge Sauroposeidon came sweeping through the area!

Branches crackled and snapped. There was a sound like an explosion, and the tree trunk shook as a heavy gray foot kicked it.

Bob wailed as the branch he clung to dipped toward the ground. His stomach lurched as he heard it splinter. Suddenly, the earth was rushing toward him.

He hit with a terrific impact, and pain flared brightly in his neck and back. He rolled several times and got up. His stomach lurching, he turned to the oncoming giant.

This Sauroposeidon wasn't alone. Two more followed it. Bob saw the other Hippies running toward him. He turned and raced away from the sauropod.

In seconds, they were again playing Twister, running while trying desperately to avoid the spots where one huge foot or another might land.

For long, exhausting minutes, Bob zigzagged through the forest. Shards of light appeared from above, revealing the sudden destruction of one tree or another.

Then—it was over.

Bob lay on the ground. He'd tripped and been covered by leaves and branches. He heard movement behind him.

He wriggled out from under the debris. The bright sun blinded him, and for a moment, he couldn't tell if the shadowy forms converging on him were Microvenators or the other Hippies.

Then he heard a cheerful array of chirps and knew that they were his friends.

His *friends?* When had he begun to think of them that way?

Bob quickly searched for the Microvenators, but he didn't see them.

What next? he thought.

Bob tried to connect with his internal "homing beacon"—the warm feeling in his stomach that usually told him if he was heading toward or away from

Ground Zero. It had faded rapidly. Yet, he recalled, when he'd been near that lake, he'd felt its pull. It was the lake where the twister had carried and then dumped him not long ago.

But how could he get back to the lake without getting trapped by the predators? Or run down by the lumbering hundred-foot-long Sauroposeidons?

For a moment, Bob thought he saw movement in the distance.

He ran and his buds followed.

After a time, they reached an area dotted with hills. Bob turned to the other Hippies and patted the closest one on the shoulder.

"You're safe now," he said. "You can go back to your homes."

The Hippies stared at him blankly.

Suddenly, a pair of shapes appeared on the horizon, cresting a small rise. Bob shoved at the Hippies, forcing them to take cover behind a pair of large rocks at the base of the hill.

He watched as the small, long-armed meat-eaters carefully scanned the area, then went back down the other side of the hill.

More Microvenators. Or members of the same pack.

"Okay," Bob said, "maybe we're just safe for now."

He spotted a cave near the crest of another hill and led the Hippies toward it. As he walked with them, Bob noticed the way that two of them would flank him, though hanging back a bit, while the others followed behind.

I've seen this before. But where?

Then it came to him. The halls of Wetherford Junior High. This was exactly the way Will Reilly's "posse" behaved!

Bob turned and stared at the other dinosaurs in surprise. They looked back at him with the same admiration Will's buddies always had in their eyes.

Bob couldn't believe it.

For the first time in his life, *he* was cool!

CHAPTER 2

PATIENCE

Patience McCray walked along a broad plain with only scattered greens dotting the region. The sail running down her back swayed in the breeze. Her claws clicked and clacked, her sharp carnivorous teeth ground.

A short time ago, she'd been the top player on Wetherford's girls' basketball team. Now she was an unhappy Acrocanthosaurus, a thirty-foot-long, vaguely T. rex–shaped juggernaut that walked, shoulders slumped, tail down, kicking at little rocks as she went.

Beside her was Zane, a long-necked Pleuro-coelus, a brontosaur, who used to be Wetherford Junior High's class clown. Runt, his long-necked baby brother, galloped around them in dizzying circles.

Runt had no previous history, as far as Patience could tell, other than being a dinosaur egg.

"It's not your fault," Zane told Patience. "You did everything you could."

"Yeah," Patience said. "I know."

She had heard this a dozen times from Zane, ever since the twister had carried off their teacher. It wasn't helping.

Without Mr. London, they had no hope of unraveling the mystery Will was facing at Ground Zero. No hope of saving the future.

No hope, period.

A wind rose up around them. Runt stopped so suddenly he nearly fell over.

"Wheeeeeeeee!" a voice called on the wind. *"This is just like riding the Cyclone!"*

"Mr. London?" Patience called. "Mr. London!"

The wind faded swiftly.

"Hey!" Zane called. "Mr. L, come back, dude, we're readin' ya loud and clear!"

But the voice did not return.

"Okay!" Patience said, brimming with excitement. "You heard it, too."

Zane's head bobbed on his incredibly long neck.

"Mr. London all right!" Patience said. "Now we just have to find him and..."

Her voice trailed off. It wasn't really her voice, in any case. The sounds that left her throat were clucks, growls, and grunts. The psychic link that all the travelers shared allowed them to hear each other's words as if they had been spoken.

Zane turned back in the direction the twister had taken.

"That thing was zigging and zagging all over the place. We could search for weeks and not find him."

The unexpected happiness that had coursed through Patience vanished altogether. "I know."

She looked at the featureless plain before her. The sun was out, and it cast a fiery glow on the horizon. Until now, they had faced nothing but rain in this new world. Soon, the hot sun would scorch them.

And if they didn't continue on, they would never reach Will in time.

"You think Mr. London'll be able to catch up with us?" Patience asked.

"Hey, this is Mr. L we're talking about. He'll figure something out."

"All right. We go on."

They walked in silence, Runt *snorfling* and making running leaps in Patience's direction—then veering off and tromping around her at the last minute.

For once, Patience didn't mind. She was filled with hope again.

Back home, Patience had a reputation for being able to take care of herself. She'd learned the hard way. She'd been abandoned by her parents when she was three, her foster mother had died when she was eight, and every friend she'd known since had abandoned or betrayed her.

People go away, she thought. *But maybe sometimes they come back.*

Maybe.

"So, do you want some more girly-girl lessons?" Zane asked.

Patience shuddered. She was, and always had been, a devoted tomboy. "I don't think so."

"Come on," Zane coaxed. "Don't you still want to get revenge on Monique?"

Patience thought about that. Monique was captain of the girls' basketball team, not because she was the best player, but because she was one of the most popular girls in school.

Because Monique was a girly-girl and Patience was not, Monique had done her best to make life difficult for Patience. Zane's girly-girl lessons were part of an elaborate plan to shut Monique up once and for all.

According to the plan, Patience was supposed to feminize her image, glam herself up, and arrive at a big party on the arm of Will Reilly, thereby shocking the most popular members of Wetherford's student body. The stunt was supposed to help Will, too. After his defeat in the election for class president, Will needed some new buzz to keep his Mr. Cool reputation going.

"No girly lessons right now," Patience said, surprising even herself. "We've got a lot of ground to cover before nightfall."

"Sure," Zane said. "Makes sense."

And it did, even if it wasn't the real reason Patience had declined Zane's offer.

The truth of it was that after meeting her dinosaur parents, Patience didn't feel quite so interested in revenge.

Her time with the Acro herd had given her something she'd never had before.

A sense of family. And belonging.

And there was one special Acrocanthosaurus, a noble being she named G.K.—short for the Green Knight. He made her feel...well, something she'd never felt before, either.

But that's over now, Patience told herself.

She wasn't about to share all this with Zane. After all, they weren't friends. They were just two people stuck together on this extended Jurassic Park ride.

And who needs all that girly-girl stuff anyway? Makeup and fashion and feminine frills. Waste of time.

They walked without chatting for nearly an hour and a half. Every now and then, Zane would do something to try and get attention. His favorite seemed to be humming the themes to old TV shows and movies.

She decided that he was trying to draw her into

some kind of game to make the boring trip that much easier to take. But she had a lot on her mind and ignored him.

Eventually, the great plain gave way to a sudden drop. Before them was a valley that had mid-size hills—mountains-in-training—on either side, like bookends.

Patience, Zane, and Runt carefully walked down into the valley. Suddenly, Patience's stomach rumbled.

Finding food had become sort of an adventure for her. She had learned to look for little holes in the ground. Small lizards burrowed into these to avoid their inevitable role as links in the food chain. Unfortunately, those critters were so tiny that she had to dig them up by the bushel to satisfy her mammoth hunger.

Patience scented a major league buffet just ahead. She ran forward, her stomach firmly in control of her mind.

What she smelled would keep her tummy happy for a day at least. Maybe more. But what could it be?

She ran on, taking a turn through the twisting range of hills. The warm glow that usually connected her to Will flared a little and stopped.

Nothing.

No, that wasn't quite right. She could smell her food. She just couldn't see it.

"Look!" Zane said, panting from his efforts to keep up with her. "Over there!"

She saw a figure struggling under fallen rocks. Her shoulders slumped in disappointment.

There goes lunch.

The half-buried creature was a fellow dinosaur. A big one. Not quite her size, but big enough. And it was alive. Not something she could eat and feel good about.

As she approached, the dinosaur's horsey face turned in her direction.

Mhrrrrrrr-urrhhhhrrrrr!

The cry was so sad. Pleading and desperate.

And filled with terror.

The trapped dinosaur struggled in vain to break free of the sheet of stone covering two-thirds of its body.

"It's a Tenontosaurus," Zane said. "A veggie-eater. Mr. L was talking about these guys."

"Not a guy," Patience said. She could sense that this was a female.

Patience heard her stomach growl again. Her pulse quickened. She bent closer—and the Tenontosaurus *swooned*.

"For heaven's sake!" Patience growled.

Runt wandered over and leaned in close, licking at the unconscious Tenontosaurus.

"We really should do something for her," Zane

said. He knocked bits of rock away with his snout.

With a sigh, Patience began digging.

"Kinda makes you feel like a paleontologist, huh?" Zane asked. "We're unearthing a dinosaur. And not some fossil, no sir—this one's alive!"

They dug, hauled rock, and dug some more, until the Tenontosaurus was free.

"She doesn't look hurt," Patience said.

"They built 'em to last back here," Zane said.

Patience sniffed. Her stomach rumbled as she scented something else. She dug through the rocks—and found another tail sticking out. A smaller tail. She batted it a few times. Nothing.

Eagerly, she heaved away the rocks covering the other dinosaur and actually found three small predators, all slightly larger than Mr. London, though they didn't look all that different from him. Except for the long arms that ended in talon-like claws.

None of them survived the rock slide that had buried the Tenontosaurus.

Patience felt saliva pooling in her maw.

Lunch was served.

Twenty delectable minutes of chewing, clawing, tearing, and swallowing later, Patience was finished.

She fell back on her tail and patted her bloated stomach. "I needed that."

The female Tenontosaurus came around just then, noticed the pile of bones beside Patience—and swooned again.

"Just as well," Patience said. "The last thing we need is fragile, little *Daisy* here following us. Runt's bad enough."

Zane, who'd just finished what looked like a healthy salad, agreed.

They left, but soon a familiar scent drifted toward them. Patience turned and saw "Daisy" following them. The Tenontosaurus froze when they turned toward her—then she hid behind a boulder.

"Oh, no...," Patience said. "This is like having Cindy following us around."

"Cindy?"

"Oh, this girl...Basketball wannabe. No real talent. A real girly-girl. She only wants to be on the team because of Monique. She figures it'll make her popular."

"Ah."

They walked on, and Zane started humming old tunes again. Patience groused and shook her head as she looked back to see Daisy moving closer.

"I mean, look at her," Patience said. "All quiet and demure. She took one look at me and passed out. She *swooned*, for heaven's sake. What a wuss."

"She may have been hit on the head," Zane said. "Head injuries—"

"Oh, yeah, like you know about stuff like that," Patience said. "Face it, 'Zane *the brain'* you're not."

Patience expected Zane to make some kind of joke, backing up what she had said. Instead, his gaze became steely and he looked a little angry.

"All I'm saying is, she's a girly-girl." Patience shrugged. "Feminine and dainty and proper. Look at the way she holds back. And she keeps her head down. Even the way she walks. It's not as bad as the stuff you were showing me with the girly-girl lessons, but still—"

"She *walks* like any plant-eating dinosaur with a reasonable fear of a predator," Zane said, cutting Patience off.

"You're not getting it."

"Clearly." He began to hum another song. This one from *The Wizard of Oz*.

"If I Only Had a Brain..."

His sour look hadn't changed in the least.

They walked on, Patience breaking into a run to lose Daisy. Zane said nothing. He simply galloped along with Runt to keep up.

Soon, Daisy's scent had vanished completely. Exactly what Patience wanted. They'd lost her.

Then, about an hour later, Patience heard something ahead.

Roars and growls.

The wind was against her, but she could still sense what was in the air.

A fight!

She raced on and came to a dark, hidden cleft in the cliff walls. In the shelter, she saw a group of the same type of small predators that had been buried with Daisy earlier.

"Microvenators!" Zane said. "The meat-eaters are Microvenators. The others were a little too banged up for a proper ID and, well, you *ate* them. But look at these!"

Patience was looking. The Microvenators were slightly larger than Mr. London and they moved with a vicious, deadly purpose. Their nasty, ripping claws and sharp teeth flashed in the near darkness. They darted about with amazing speed, slashing and biting at something.

That's when Patience realized—that *something* was another Tenontosaurus.

The plant-eater struggled, hurling one of the predators against a nearby wall and stunning it. There was a mad, defiant glare in its eyes. The dinosaur growled, spit, kicked, and smashed at the attacking meat-eaters.

Patience respected *this* dinosaur. The way it moved, the way it fought. This one was nothing like Dainty Daisy. She couldn't bear the thought of this one falling.

But what should she do to help?

What *could* she do?

If Patience went into the cave, the little meat-eaters would probably swarm over Zane and Runt.

The wind kicked up. A draft whipped around the confines of the small enclosure and reached Patience. She sniffed and couldn't believe what she was smelling.

"Daisy," Patience said excitedly. "Zane, that's *Daisy!*"

"She must have taken a passage through the mountains to come out ahead of us," he guessed. "But—why?"

From the dim shadows of the recess came the answer. Lumbering and hurt, another Tenontosaurus appeared.

A male. Daisy's *mate.*

At the sight of the easier kill, the Microvenators fled from Daisy. Or—they tried to.

Daisy was on them with a swiftness Patience never would have expected. She grabbed two of the meat-eaters by the backs of their necks, lifted them high, and smacked their skulls together.

The one she'd stunned earlier was on his feet, scrambling toward the male. Daisy kicked. There was a sharp crackle of impact and the predator lay on his back, his little arms and legs kicking, then growing still.

Two more meat-eaters raced beyond her. She launched herself forward and fell on one, tackling it like a football.

It—*squished.*

But the other one was free. It sped toward the dazed, injured male.

"NO!" Patience screamed.

The sound that actually emerged from her was a

roar made even louder by the cave's small space.

The Microvenator and the male Tenontosaurus both froze. Daisy turned wearily. Her gaze narrowed as it fixed on Patience.

And Patience took a step back.

That was all the Microvenator needed to see. It circled far and wide around the male and vanished down a slim, dark tunnel.

"Hey, that was cool!" Zane said. "Backing up when you did. Making the Microvenators think even *you* were scared of Daisy. Using your head. And not just—"

"She *looked* scary," Patience said. "She still looks scary."

"Maybe we should leave now."

"Maybe."

And they did.

They walked for a time, following their route. Patience still felt like she was in shock.

"Okay if I mention something?" Zane asked, looking at her with his dark eyes.

"Uh-huh."

"You look wigged."

Patience considered. "Uh-huh."

"Any particular reason?"

Patience picked up the pace a little. "Just...Daisy. Dainty Daisy May. She just kicked some serious booty."

"Yes, she did."

"But she's a girly-girl."

"I guess...," Zane said. "The way I figure it, she must have been forced to leave her mate behind to go look for grub. Then she was cornered by Microvenators and trapped by the rock slide."

"She didn't need us rescuing her."

"I don't think so. But, what do I know, right? Zane *the brain* I'm not."

Patience had actually noticed Zane using his brains a lot more lately than she ever would have thought possible. A part of her decided that maybe she owed him an apology.

But she was a lot more interested in what she had seen with Daisy. For some reason, it made her feel happy.

As confused as before, but happy.

CHAPTER 3

WILL

Arbuckle Mountains, Oklahoma
112 million years ago

Far away from Patience and Zane, in a maze of underground caverns, Will Reilly was trapped. And fighting for his life—or, at least, for the life of the raptor he now inhabited, a Deinonychus to be precise.

Will stumbled back as another raptor, the one he'd named Hook, flew at him. The other raptor had a red body and amber and turquoise spots. Hook snarled and bit as he raised his one good leg and slashed with his sickle claw.

With a cry of pain, Hook fell back, his wounded limb unable to support his weight. He hit the ground hard, then scrambled on his knees toward the underground chamber's *third* inhabitant.

Tink was a Tenontosaurus that Will had befriended. The two of them had been trapped together in these underground tunnels. And, even though she was a plant-eater, it seemed she had started to trust Will.

But not anymore.

Not since Hook had shown up, tumbling down from the gap way up in the cavern's high ceiling.

Now Tink was in a panic. And Will knew why.

Hook was *all* raptor *all* the time. There was no humanity inside this dinosaur. Just the TEAR-SLASH-KILL that HUNGRY-HUNGRY predators communicated when they saw vulnerable prey.

Will also knew why Tink had moved her large body to block the only other gap leading outside of the chamber. That floor-level gap led to a maze of tunnels—and one of those tunnels led to an even larger chamber where the rest of Tink's herd had been trapped.

Of course, another tunnel, a closer one, led to what Will called "the lizard room." It was full of tiny, green salamander-like prey.

But Tink wasn't taking any chances that Hook would stop at the lizard room and not move on to her herd. It was pretty clear that she would let him get to her family only one way—over her dead body. Will watched as she bravely stared at Hook, daring him to attack.

Moving quickly, Will leaped onto Hook's back.

But the injured raptor slowly crawled on.

Will growled and bit at the back of the other raptor's neck. He brought his arm around as if they were wrestling and he were trying to pin Hook, but the Deinonychus reared up and flung him off.

Will hissed and leaped on Hook again. This time, he took the other dinosaur from the side. Hook struggled and kicked furiously with his sickle claw. But the

ferocious raptor was belly down and couldn't maneuver into a position to do Will any harm.

This is crazy, Will thought. *What am I supposed to do, hold on to him forever?*

Will had to make some move, a show of strength that Hook would respect. Something to get Hook under control and keep him that way.

The flickering golden light from Will's torch cast terrifying shadows across the chamber walls.

Long before Hook had tumbled down into the chamber, Will had figured out how to make a torch out of the materials around him.

For the torch's handle, he'd used a length of hard root. For the flammable top, he'd used dry vines and leaves that had been buried by the earthquake. Stone and flint had allowed him to create the spark that ignited the dry kindling.

When Hook had tumbled into the chamber, Will had been so startled, he'd dropped the torch. Now its light cast shadowy shapes of two grappling inhuman creatures.

He was one of them.

The torch hissed and sparked, making the shadows broaden, lengthen, then withdraw.

The torch! That's it!

Will kicked Hook in the belly, then leaped off the raptor. He raced to the torch, picked it up, and spun.

Hook was almost on Tink!

With a single leap, Will bounded to the injured raptor and brushed the torch against Hook's foot.

"Yie-yi-yi-yi-yieeeeee!"

Hook spun away, rolling on his side. He rose on his uninjured leg, his claws scraping the wall behind him. The wounded raptor leaned against the wall and struggled to bring his twisted leg around. He hissed and snapped at the air separating him from Will and the torch.

Hook had learned a healthy respect for the flames.

"I need you to listen to me," Will said, desperate to try anything to reach the raptor. "Whatever you're thinking—"

Hook charged, startling Will so much he almost dropped the torch. Hook shoved off from the wall, clearly trying to spring into a great leap. But the injured raptor fell far short of Tink.

The Tenontosaurus howled in rage and surged forward, kicking the stunned, confused raptor. Hook was lifted off the ground by the kick. His body snapped backward and he fell onto his back, his trembling sickle claw raised.

Will now scented the other raptor's fear.

Tink backed away from the glinting claw.

Will moved into position between them. But this time, he had to wave the torch both at Hook *and* Tink, refereeing their conflict.

He gazed at the glaring hatred in Tink's eyes. It wasn't just for Hook. Raptors had hunted her pack. Driven them to hiding in these mountains. Then a rock slide had sealed them in.

All but Tink had reached a vast underground cave where there was food and water. But the herd couldn't last forever. Starvation loomed on the horizon for Tink and her kind.

"Come on, both of you," Will said, breathing hard. "It doesn't have to be like this."

Deep down, he wondered if that was true. Could he make a difference? Could he somehow make this meat-eater and plant-eater, these natural enemies, see each other in a different light?

His dad, good old "Briefcase Man," always said, *Don't wait for things to change. Change them yourself.*

That was easy to say. But how could he make it happen? And *quickly?*

The flames were keeping the wounded raptor and the hulking Tenontosaurus at bay. But what would happen when the torch went out?

Will looked at Hook. "You're the big problem. I was doing okay with her until you showed up."

Hook retreated until he was sitting with his back against the wall, favoring his hurt leg. Will couldn't tell if it was broken or sprained. But he could feel the pain the other dinosaur was suffering.

Hook hissed and spat. He yipped and screamed.

His tail whipped about. He bit and clawed helplessly in the direction of the wailing Tenontosaurus.

But he didn't attempt to rise.

Without thinking, Will unsheathed his own sickle claws. Hook froze. He stared at Will anxiously.

Then Hook howled in anguish.

Something stirred deep within Will. He had an idea of what Hook was thinking. *We're the same. Predators. Raptors. We even come from the same pack. We shouldn't be fighting.*

Though he was ashamed to admit it, the thought had crossed Will's mind, too.

Will advanced on Hook and kicked out with one of his sickle claws. The wounded raptor gasped and withdrew.

Then, like someone caught in a lie, he stared at Will. Hook's hunger and his pain and his need for self-preservation all seemed to be at war inside him. Hook seemed confused at what to do next.

It was the opening Will needed.

"All right," Will said. "We're getting out of here."

He turned to Tink. The Tenontosaurus was still guarding the gateway to the vast maze of tunnels and caverns beyond.

"I'm sorry," he whispered.

Will hurled the torch at Tink. The Tenontosaurus darted out of the way of the fiery object. Before the torch had even struck the wall where Tink had stood,

Will surged forward, grabbing Hook's shoulders. He yanked the other raptor up and flung him toward the opening. Then he kicked and bit and chased Tink through it.

Tink howled and came flying back toward him. Will missed a swipe of her claws by inches!

"Move, move!" Will shouted. He punctuated his yells with snaps from his maw and swipes of his own claws.

Hook didn't hesitate. In seconds, the rich heady smells of prey came to them. It was coming from the chamber Will had nicknamed "the lizard room."

Hook yelped in delight. He rushed ahead, flinging himself forward into the darkness.

"Wait, wait!" Will yelled, trying to warn the raptor of the drop he was facing. But Hook's hunger had taken hold, outweighing all other considerations. Will could feel it!

HUNGRY-HUNGRY-HUNGRY

From the dim flickering of his torch at the mouth of the tunnel behind them, Will could see Hook's tail as it struck excitedly from side to side. Then the raptor dropped out of sight with a sharp yelp.

There was a thump, a slight moan. And then the frenzied sounds of feasting.

Will looked over the edge. In the dim light, he could see Hook thrashing about, snatching up small, green salamander-like creatures and stuffing them into his mouth. Will sat with his feet dangling over the edge, watching the dinosaur. It was difficult to resist the temptation to join him.

At least, Hook didn't hurt himself worse, Will thought.

He didn't want harm to come to Hook, or Tink, or anyone else.

Yet...

"I wonder what the Big Guy would say if he could see you right now," Will murmured.

He thought of all that had happened since he came to the age of dinosaurs. The trials he had put himself through to gain the approval of Big Guy, the pack leader—only to win the older raptor's respect when he stopped caring one way or another.

Below, Hook eased up on his feeding frenzy. He gazed up at Will with something that might have been gratitude.

Hook motioned at the food and inclined his head.

We should share. It could be just like you wanted it to be. We could be equals. Partners.

"How'd you get down here, anyway?" Will asked. "Were you curious? Did you smell Tink when you shoved *me* down the rabbit hole? Or did your friends up there turn on you and decide to shove *you* down here, too?"

Hook went back to his meal.

Will thought of his human life and the one thing

that had always been the most important to him: being popular, being liked.

Like Hook.

Will knew that if Hook got out of here...And if he led the raptor pack to the Tenontosaurus herd...

Well, there was no doubt that Big Guy would be impressed. Hook's place in the pack would be high, even with his injury.

And what about me? thought Will. *If I end up here for the rest of my life, what am I going to do?*

Will knew that he might fail at doing what Bertram had advised. He might not be able to stop whatever was going to happen here at Ground Zero tomorrow.

Then what?

Then I'll have to consider doing exactly what Hook was going to do. I'll have to consider how to secure my place in the pack.

For my own survival.

Hook looked up from his meal, jabbering happily. It seemed clear what he was saying: *Dude, you really should try some of this. It rocks!*

But Will had no appetite. The thoughts he was wrestling with made his stomach churn.

Sometime tomorrow, he would have to make a choice.

It wouldn't be an easy one.

CHAPTER 4

BOB

When Bob London first encountered the small group of Hypsilophodons, he had barely been able to tell one from another. They all had the same drab gray-green coloring, were roughly the same size, with no features to mark the individual Hippie.

Yet...

While he sat with them, trying to come up with a plan for reaching the waters and crossing the vast lake, he had begun to detect differences among them.

First, there was Leo. The creative one.

While the three others sat around bored, waiting for something to happen, Leo came up with games for them to play. One game was like hot potato.

The Hippie who was "it" had to tag one of the others with both claws to "pass it on." He got them to run races and to see how high each could jump. He made a contest out of foraging to motivate the others.

Bob named him for Leonardo da Vinci.

Then there was Albert, the great thinker.

He had a real knack for getting others to do his work for him. When it came time to forage, he convinced them that he had a sore foot—an injury that conveniently disappeared a short time later. When it was his turn to be the lookout, he became nearsighted, squinting, walking into walls, stumbling along as if he didn't see sudden drops along the cliffside.

He wasn't *exactly* Albert Einstein, but he'd do.

Carl, the dreamer, was the next one.

While it was possible that he simply liked to stare off into space, Bob had a sense, more often than not, that Carl was studying the clouds and the heavens for a reason. He felt that Carl was captivated by the land and what might lay beyond.

Once, he saw Carl picking up a branch and waving it like a sword—the way Bob had when the Microvenators attacked. Then he'd drop it and pretend to be one of the Microvenators! Only it was more of a parody of the predators, his arms dangling and wavering, his head wiggling from one side to another while his mouth hung open drooling and his eyes rolled.

He was *pretending*—looking at things from more than one point of view.

Then Carl would sit and look up at the sky with an

expression of wonder, curiosity, and sadness.

Bob felt that he had the soul of an explorer. A philosopher. He thought that if Carl Sagan were here, this is the little Hippie in which he'd be most interested.

Finally, there was Hal.

He was easily annoyed, and the others picked on him for just that reason. He liked things neat and orderly.

Hal cleaned his place before he sat down. He licked his fingers after eating. He didn't like Albert's lazy and crafty ways, and he didn't appreciate Carl's sense of wonder or Leo's inventiveness.

This was a dinosaur ruled by logic. At least, until he became too frustrated. Then he would leap and wrestle with the others, and afterward sullenly take a resting place away from the others.

He reminded Bob of the computer from the movie *2001: A Space Odyssey*, the computer called HAL— the logical intellect that went a little wonky from time to time.

The Hippies all treated Bob in a way he had never been treated before. He was both one of them and looked up to by them.

They brought him food and water. When he felt excited, they became happy. When he grew sad, they tried to make him laugh or distract him.

It was in these little moments, when Bob London

wasn't trying so hard, that answers came to him.

He now had an idea for getting to the lake without attracting the attention of the Microvenators. But he still had another problem to work through.

Since he had hit a wall with that, he decided to tell the Hippies a story.

"This is how I remember it," Bob said, his companions gathered around him. "A young boy sat on a high cliff at dawn, listening to tales spun by his grandfather. He was told that if he could reach the spot where the rainbows end, he would find a golden key.

"The boy asked, 'What door does this key open?' And his grandfather said, 'That is what you must find out.'"

Bob stopped and frowned.

"Funny. That's all I can remember. But...I had an *amber* key in my hand just this morning, and I could sense it unlocked the future itself.

"The how or why, I don't know. But for some time now, I've known that there are doors. Gateways to other worlds—other times, really. And I was desperate to open them and step on through to the other side."

The Hippies hung on his every word. Bob stood and walked to the mouth of the cave. "Now I'm wondering why."

He laughed. Here he was, acting like he was back

in the classroom, lecturing to a group of students.

Well, these weren't students. They obviously considered themselves friends—which made what he had to do even harder.

Suddenly, the answer he had been seeking came to him.

"Gentlemen," Bob said, turning to face the Hippies, "I think it's time I taught you a new game!"

Leo and the others leaped around excitedly. Bob scanned the horizon, checking for threats. Seeing none, he began.

The game was hide-and-seek. It took some time to teach the Hypsilophodons the rules. They wanted desperately to follow him, so he had to make Leo "it" in the beginning. But soon they caught on, and by the fifth round, all four Hippies stood in a huddle with their eyes closed while Bob raced away from them.

Bob scrambled through the forest and came to a stream he'd spotted from above. He rolled around in the mud near the bank until the muck covered him completely.

Then he went on his way, confident that the others would be trailing him by scent—as he had taught them—and not by signs like broken twigs or pawprints.

He was miles away, running hard, when he heard movement from a cluster of trees ahead.

Bob ducked under a heavy, curling root and watched as a pair of saurian legs leaped over the root and continued on.

He worried for an instant that the Microvenators had come back, that he had led the other Hippies right into their path.

No, it was Hal and Albert working together. They raced on, sniffing the air, shrugging in confusion. Bob waited until they were long gone before he continued making his way to the lake.

As he scurried along, Bob felt the first twinges of guilt. He liked Leo and the other Hippies. He didn't enjoy ditching them, even if it *was* for their own good. After all, allowing them to follow him to Ground Zero would be irresponsible. He had no idea what dangers waited there.

But he also felt lonely. *That* was crazy, of course. He had pretty much been on his own all his life. He had been a "boy genius," sent to college when he was fifteen. His grades, his grasp of advanced scientific theories, and his absolute lack of any social graces had conspired to set him apart. He had no friends, only students who wanted things from him.

Was that what life had been like for Will? Bob wondered.

No, he decided. Will was comfortable in his own skin, something Bob had never been.

Ahead, the sweet smells of the lake reached him.

Only—he wasn't alone.

Bob scrambled up a series of low branches until he had climbed to the upper reaches of a forty-foot tree. Cautiously, he crept out onto a sturdy branch and surveyed the lake.

A trio of thirty-foot-long dinosaurs stood at the edge of the water. The dinosaurs walked hunched over on their rear legs, like a couple of T. rexes. Their large bodies were thick with muscle. Their tails were long and heavy, tapering off to a sharp point. Their necks were a foot or two long, their heads slightly egg-shaped.

But their most arresting feature was one they probably would have been arrested *for,* had the fashion police been around—their scales.

They had the funkiest array of multicolored racing stripes Bob had ever seen. Zigzag patterns of white, purple, gold, pink, yellow, orange, and bright lime-green zoomed along their forms.

The way the lines went over the first one's head made him look like he wore a Lone Ranger mask. And the other dinosaurs looked bright enough to glow in the dark.

They were funny-looking. Totally non-threatening. Except for one thing—their claws.

Bob squinted when he saw the huge killer spikes that rose from each of their hands. Sunlight glinted off the razor-tipped edges.

Iguanodons.

Peaceful enough plant-eaters who could *defend* themselves in a scrap.

Bob thought of Zane and his silly way of naming the dinosaurs he encountered. In honor of the absent student, Bob decided to call the trio Spike, Sluggo, and Speed Racer.

The branch upon which he'd been resting suddenly snapped. Bob wailed as he dropped through a net of branches and leaves, hitting the ground and suffering a sore shoulder and bottom but no other damage.

The noise had been enough to make the Iggies look his way.

"Hi, guys," Bob said. "I wonder if I could ask a favor?"

The Iggies snuffled and turned back to the shore, where they snacked on bits of seaweed.

Bob wondered if there was something he could offer the Iguanodons, some way he could get them to pitch in with the work he had planned. It would certainly go quicker if he had help.

"I don't suppose any of you has a thorn stuck in his paw or anything like that?" Bob asked.

The Iggies did not choose to dignify the question with a reply.

Bob felt like a freshman again, still not fitting in with the bigger students.

Suddenly, a rustling came from behind. A group of dark shapes sprang from the cover of the forest and pounced on Bob. He yelped, certain the Microvenators had found him, then sighed with relief as he felt lapping little tongues and playful little claws swatting at him.

Leo, Hal, Albert, and Carl had learned the game a lot better than Bob had ever expected!

He sighed as he rolled away from them. "All right. I guess you can help after all."

He went into the woods and scoured the paths for logs of just the right size. The other Hippies, certain this was some new fun game, followed him without the slightest pause.

"Well, class," Bob said, "today we're going to build a raft..."

CHAPTER 5

ZANE

Zane was trudging along the outskirts of a lush forest when Patience nudged him.

"Do you notice something?" she asked.

"If you're going to say 'It's quiet, *too* quiet,' I promise I'll scream like I'm in a cheesy horror movie."

Patience hesitated. "But it is, isn't it?"

Zane hated to admit it, but she was right. He looked around, scanning for predators.

Nothing.

Not even—

"*Runt!*" Looking back along his flanks, Zane was startled to see that the baby bronto was gone. He turned to Patience. "I thought you were watching him!"

She raised the long sliver of amber that hadn't left her claw since she'd returned from the Acrocanthosaurus clan.

"I'm watching *this*," she replied. "Bertram said we needed it to set everything right and get home. He didn't say anything about Runt."

Zane was furious. "You let him run off?"

She shook her head. "I didn't let him do anything. You weren't paying attention, either."

"I thought you were!"

She flung her tiny arms upward. "I thought *you* were!"

Zane squeezed his eyes shut and banged his head against the trunk of a nearby tree.

"Listen," Patience said, her tone a little softer. "We were heading someplace dangerous anyway. What were we going to do, take him all the way to Ground Zero? He belongs to this time. He—"

Zane opened his eyes and brushed past Patience, sniffing, trying to pick up Runt's distinctive scent.

"Are you serious?" she asked.

"We've got to find him."

"Why?"

Zane's gaze narrowed. "He's family. I don't know if you can understand that or not, but he is, so we are, and that's it."

His heart thundered. He felt certain Patience would roar with rage and perhaps even abandon him right there on the spot.

Instead, she nodded slowly. "Okay. I know his scent, too. This'll go faster if we work together."

Zane was startled. "Thanks. I mean—"

"Don't push it."

He didn't. Patience had made her opinion clear when she and Mr. London first met up with him. She didn't think he'd be of use in a pinch. To Patience, Zane would always be a clown, not a hero.

Back then, Mr. London had to talk her into coming along, telling her that she would have to protect the group—just like Will and Lance had always protected Zane back at Wetherford.

But Zane noticed that something about Patience had changed since she returned from retrieving the stolen key from the Acro clan. She hadn't been *quite* so hostile and unwavering as before.

Zane wished he knew what had really happened, but for now he was simply grateful that she wasn't fighting him.

As they tracked Runt, they also smelled the tingling, pleasant scent of fresh water. They had found ponds left by the frequent downpours, and Zane had depleted a few of them in his travels. But this scent was different.

This water was flowing and brimming with life—

A river!

If Runt was lost and not playing, he would be drawn to the water, perhaps to find other long-neck herds on the shore.

Zane and Patience climbed a hill and saw the snaking zigzag of the river far below. It was wider than he'd expected, and there was something at its heart—a little island that the waters flowed around. He saw movement on that island. A large form frolicking among a host of smaller ones...

Runt!

"Hey, buddy!" Zane called as he happily lumbered down the slope, into the river valley.

Pterosaurs circled above the island, sailing down at Runt, then veering in Zane's direction.

"I wonder if one of them will land on me?" Zane said. "That would be great!"

"Can we just get Runt and go?" Patience asked.

The pterosaurs soared toward them. "Come on, you've gotta admit, it's pretty cool."

"I'm reminded of chicken wings. The spicy kind."

Zane refused to let Patience's bad attitude ruin this experience for him. He watched the fliers for a time before he noticed three of them were flying really low.

Up close, they didn't look like the other pterosaurs he'd seen, either.

These creatures had ugly beaks with weird, round bowls as the ends of their jaws. Crooked, nasty teeth spiked out of their beaks, and their eyes burned with fury. Their wings whipped and flapped as they poured on more speed, to become streaking, screaming gold, crimson, and purple blurs.

And they were diving right for his head!

"Whahhhhh!" Zane cried, ducking.

Through his amazing peripheral vision, he saw the living, breathing B-52s sail down on his flank, reaching out to rake their claws into his scales.

Zane whipped his tail—

CRRRRRR-RRRRRACCKKKKKKKKKK!

And the startled fliers broke formation, zipping in alarm to safety.

"What is your *problem?*" Zane hollered.

"Good question," Patience said. Even she looked a little unnerved. But that was probably because of the tail crack. The sound scared her inner dino.

The fliers cawed and came around for another attack run. This time Patience roared at them. They pulled up and made a wide arc around the pair.

Zane and Patience walked closer to the little island. The fliers above cawed a warning and went back to dive-bombing Runt. The little dino was prancing about, smashing eggshells and playfully chasing tiny little pterosaur hatchlings.

"They're chicks. Too small to fly," Patience cried. "They must be, or else they'd have gotten away from Runt by now."

"It's a rookery. You know, day care for baby birds," Zane said. "The adults can go into the air to avoid trouble. But not the little ones. All they have is the waters around the island for protection."

"Against what? If Runt could walk over there, then an Acro like me could do it, too."

"Something smaller, I guess," Zane said. "Maybe those Microvenators who were after Daisy."

"Yeah."

Zane watched as the baby brontosaurus leaned his head close to a weird-looking beaky baby, then pulled away. He did it again and again.

I'm not touching you, Runt seemed to be teasing.

"Great. He learns from the best," Patience said.

"What?"

"Come on, Zane. You were doing that to me and Mr. London yesterday."

"Oh. Right."

For a moment, Zane thought he smelled something new. Something small and light and unfamiliar and—

HUNGRY-HUNGRY-HUNGRY

But there was nothing in sight. Probably just a couple of the Microvenators, Zane decided.

Well, if it came down to it, Patience could handle them. He pictured a handful of Mr. Londons attacking her. He forced back a laugh.

"Yo, Runt!" Zane called. "Time to get going. Come on back!"

Runt ignored him.

"I guess you'll just have to go over there and get him," Patience said.

Zane looked at the rushing waters. He suddenly felt very frightened. "Why me?"

"I'd scare the little ones," Patience said. "They'd probably dive into the river and get carried downstream."

Zane remembered the sharks and other weird things he'd seen in the waters near the shore, where he had first "landed" in the Mesozoic. He suddenly realized he was shifting his massive weight from one leg to the other, as if he were trying to get a hall pass.

He was a wuss, and he knew it.

He also hated it.

"I'm goin'," Zane said.

He shuddered, then took the plunge. His belly grumbled as he waded into the rising waters. The current was fierce, worse than he'd expected. But he could still cross it without difficulty.

Looking down, he saw that the island was *shrinking*. Its outer perimeter was being swallowed up by the waters, leaving a smaller and smaller ring at the center.

All the hatchlings were grouped there now.

He looked up and saw the waters pouring in from upriver. The storm may have ended here, but up north, it looked like it was still going on.

All that rainwater was heading this way.

"Patience, we've gotta get these guys out of here!" Zane called.

She didn't answer. But the trio of pterosaurs circling above cawed wildly. Zane looked back and froze.

A pair of small, nasty-looking dinosaurs raced at Patience from either side. They were about the size of human beings. Curved, little sickle claws unsheathed from the feet.

Raptors.

Fear gripped Zane, but he fought it.

"Patience, get in the water! Mr. London said raptors had fragile bodies—they won't be able to cross!"

Nodding, Patience stumbled back into the froth.

Okay, okay, we're doin' good, we're fine, we're—

He looked ahead and saw a trio of raptors on the *other* shore.

Waiting.

Zane treaded softly toward the island, his massive heart ready to burst as he desperately tried to come up with a plan.

But he wasn't having much luck.

Zane slogged through the waters. He was halfway to the island when the raptors on the shore began yipping and squealing. Zane saw that they were racing around in anxious, expectant circles.

It had been scary enough when the meat-eaters had just been standing there, maws open wide, eyes glaring. Now they were frantic, frenzied, *loud* blurs of motion, and it was becoming a lot harder for Zane to consider doing anything other than screaming in fear.

But he had to keep moving. He didn't have a choice. The waters were still rising, and before long the pterosaur rookery would be completely sub-merged—the young fliers carried downriver and drowned—unless he got them to safety first.

Safety, uh-huh. That's likely, thought Zane. This whole place had suddenly become a red-hot raptor hangout!

The scene before him was painted with lush, beautiful colors. The deep blue of the sky, the elec-tric green of the forest, the soft tan and white sands of the shore, the sparkling lighter blue waters, and the crimson streaks of the runaway raptors.

It was all stunning. And all the more terrible because of the danger all around them.

Above, the older fliers pierced the air with their helpless screams of alarm.

"Come on! Do something!" Zane yelled. "They're *your* kids!"

Just then, the lead flier sailed down and swept around Zane. The pterosaur's great wings were framed in the sunlight, and Zane saw how thin and fragile the fliers really were.

They had puny bodies and hollow bones. There was no way the pterosaurs had the strength to lift their young and fly away with them.

The current was strengthening now. Zane turned to look at the baby pterosaurs huddled at the center of the island.

Runt stood in front of the rookie flying squadron, shading the squawking batch of beak-faces with his VW-size bulk. He didn't look the least bit afraid.

Lucky him.

Zane plodded forward, making his way to the edge of the partially submerged island. There wasn't a lot of room for him. His legs and underbelly were still in the water.

He stepped up, onto the ground. His head bobbed a few yards above the rookery and Runt.

So now what?

"Zane, we can't stay here!" Patience shouted.

He looked back. She was beginning to lose it.

It occurred to Zane that Patience was looking to him for answers. If that was true, then he couldn't let her down. Not her or Runt or the fliers—or even himself.

Not this time.

He had to *do* something, no matter how scared he was.

Suddenly, he had an idea.

Zane looked to the far shore, where only two raptors waited. He concentrated and allowed his imagination to run wild.

An entire herd of large zebra-striped Iguanodons

appeared behind the raptors. Their colors were wild, their patterns bold and striking. Their scents were rich and overpowering, even from where Zane stood. And every one of the spikes on their thumbs had been shaved down to soft, round, little bumps.

The raptors spun and chased after the mental projections. The phony Iguanodons fled south with astounding speed. In seconds, the raptors were tiny blurs. The Iggies darted into the woods and the raptors followed.

"You did it!" Patience yelled. She splashed through the waters behind him.

The little pterosaurs stared at her in terror.

Zane had another idea. He lowered his head and sent his visions into the minds of the adult fliers circling above. They landed, flapping their heavy wings, and shepherded their young onto Zane's head and neck. Zane felt a little tickling as the junior flight squadron settled into place, then he turned to Runt. The baby brontosaurus stared at him excitedly.

Zane knew that look.

"We'll play *later*," Zane said sternly.

Runt sighed and followed as Zane walked across the island and headed into the currents on the other side.

The crossing was difficult, but Zane kept his balance and his concentration. Soon, he and Runt were on the shore. Zane lowered his head and the waddling, little fliers disembarked.

"Hope you enjoyed your flight. Your movie today was *Iggies A-Go-Go* or *Runaway Raptors!* We hope you enjoyed the entertainment."

Zane was still shaking, but he'd kept the images and the smells of the Iguanodons fixed firmly in his mind. The striped dinosaurs were running and running, and they wouldn't stop running until Zane went to sleep tonight.

It was safe. He'd done it!

He turned back to see the rising waters flow over the rookery, carrying broken shells out with the current that slapped against the shore. Patience was slogging her way through the waters. She looked amazed.

He winked at her. "So who said I wasn't the brains of this outfit, huh?"

Zane paused.

Patience wasn't looking at him with the kind of admiration he'd expected. In fact, she had stiffened and was looking down the shoreline.

YIEEEEEEE-YIP-YIP-YIP-YIP-YIP

HUNGRY-HUNGRY-HUNGRY

Zane's entire body tensed as he saw them—two scarlet blurs racing back from downriver.

The raptors.

But—it didn't make sense! What about the Iggies? The in-flight movie was still running—fresh, juicy scents and all! He still had the dinosaurs racing and racing and—

And moving *right through* anything in their path like the ghostly, unreal things they were.

"No," Zane whispered. He coiled his tail instinctively. "No..."

HUNGRY-HUNGRY-HUNGRY

He'd seen raptors in movies and documentaries at school. He knew what they could do to a slow-moving target like himself. And precisely how quickly they could do it.

He forced Runt away. The little dinosaur tried to move in front of him, barking fiercely at the raptors, but Zane cracked his whip tail.

CRRRRRR-RACCCKKKK!

The terrible sound made Runt back away, while the pterosaurs fled with their young.

The raptors had veered off and raced into the forest, frightened by the sound, but Zane knew they'd be back.

Patience crawled out of the water, her legs sinking into the soft sand. "We should look for rocks we can throw at them. Or branches, shells—anything we can use to get them!"

Zane shuddered. His fear was back, and it was overwhelming.

"Zane, you did good," Patience said. "Now stay with me!"

She sounded afraid, too. But she was obviously determined to fight the raptors.

Zane found a heavy rock embedded in the shore. He picked it up in his maw and tossed it as the first of the raptors reappeared.

The rock thumped to the sand with a big, wet *splorch,* falling a good fifteen feet short of the first predator.

Zane couldn't control it any longer. The fear took over.

They're gonna get me, they're gonna get me! Zane's mind chanted.

He saw the raptors break left and right, one coming for each of his flanks, and he squeezed his eyes shut!

Zane, honey, you've got power! the Psychic Friends Network hollered from inside him. *Use it! Think!*

But he couldn't think. He wailed and howled in fear, crying and screaming and waiting for it to start hurting!

Nothing started hurting.

Instead, he heard grunts of exertion mingled with yips of surprise. Then a thud, a wailing that dwindled, and a soft, wet sound he couldn't identify.

"Well, at least you didn't pull the covers over your head this time," Patience said.

Zane opened his eyes. He saw one of the raptors being swept downriver.

The other had been driven like a nail right into the wet sand! He was buried up to his nipping, biting, and very confused head.

Runt stood over him, his entire left flank covered in white wet sand.

"I tossed a couple of rocks and knocked the one into the river," Patience said. "Runt took care of the other one. He just kinda hopped on the guy and squished him down into the sand."

Patience gazed at the fearless baby long-neck. "You know, kid, you've got possibilities."

Suddenly, Zane thought about the first time Patience had seen Zane back here, in the age of dinosaurs. He'd been running from a green and brown Acro, with the illusion of his childhood "blankie" over his head.

He had looked pitiful then, and he felt pitiful now.

"Hey, you *could* say thank you," Patience said to Zane. "We did just save your life."

Zane looked to the pterosaurs, which he had saved, flying away in the distance.

Not one mention of that, thought Zane. *Nothing.*

"Thanks," he said, turning away.

They walked on—Runt holding his head high alongside Patience; Zane trailing far, far behind.

CHAPTER 6

WILL

Will stared into Hook's eyes as he fastened the last of the bindings. He had made a splint that held Hook's injured leg in the proper position so the raptor could walk—or at least hobble.

Mad leaps or furious battles, on the other hand, were out of the question.

The Deinonychus, who had been wary about letting Will come close to him at first, had unsheathed his sickle claw.

When Will didn't back down, Hook had slowly withdrawn it. Will had seized the raptor's leg and straightened it so quickly that Hook had yipped and passed out from the pain.

That made the rest of Will's work much easier.

Vines and branches were all he had for materials, but they were enough.

When Hook woke up, he saw the splint Will was placing on him and struggled for a moment.

Then he seemed to realize that his pain was less

since Will set the broken limb. After that, the raptor had allowed Will to continue.

Will thought long and hard about doing this for the raptor. He believed that Hook would betray him the first chance he got.

The solution was simple. Will wouldn't give Hook that chance.

And *that* meant keeping the raptor close while Will continued to explore the tunnels.

"Try and stand," Will said, backing away from the raptor.

Hook looked down at his leg and pushed off against the wall behind him. He put most of his weight on his good leg, only a little on the injured one.

He winced, as if in great pain. Then he hissed and bared his crooked-toothed maw, as if to say it didn't matter.

"Good," Will said. "Then let's go."

Will raised a torch and led the hobbling raptor from the lizard room to one of the branching tunnels he hadn't yet explored. He created a new system of marks to tell this tunnel apart from the ones he had already explored.

It wasn't long before he sensed that they were being followed.

Another predator was loose in the tunnels. Will had caught only a glimpse of it the last time he had been exploring. It was a long-armed meat-eater with raking fingers and a smaller body than Will's.

It wasn't bold enough to go after Tink. But Will could easily picture it in the vast underground lair of the Tenontosaurus herd, looking to pick off one of the younger dinosaurs trapped below with their elders.

The other predator had saved Will's life, though not on purpose.

Will had been about to enter a chamber filled with gas, his torch held high. The resulting explosion would have reduced him to ashes.

The predator had knocked the torch from his hand just in time.

"I think our friend wanted to warn me off," Will said to Hook. "Maybe he wanted me to know this was his territory. Now he's following us. Might be drawn by the light. Or it might be something else. I dunno. You have any ideas?"

Hook grunted.

"I'd like to know if he's alone. I wish I could think of some way of finding out."

Hook turned and hissed into the darkness. Footsteps padded off.

After a few seconds, they returned.

Will tilted his head slightly. "That was a good move. Now we know he might be cautious around us, but he's not scared. There're two of us, one of him, but he isn't afraid. Maybe he *does* have friends."

Hook sniffed the air. The tunnels branched ahead of them. Hook sneezed.

The air was dusty and close. The clean air circulating through the tunnels wasn't coming from this direction.

Hook turned. His gaze narrowed. He started back.

Will was about to call out to the raptor, to remind him who was in charge. But his instinct was to follow Hook.

Until the accident that had cost him one of his prized sickle claws, Hook had been known as Junior. The chosen one of the Big Guy, the raptor pack leader. He had done everything he could to make Will's life among the raptors a nightmare.

But now, as he walked beside Hook—taking it very slowly, so he never showed his back to the other dinosaur—Will was reminded of walking down the halls at school with his buddy Lance at his side.

It felt comfortable in some ways, but scary in others.

I'm starting to feel like one of them, Will thought. *A raptor.*

He shuddered.

Hook and Will followed the other predator. Will thrust his torch forward, trying to see more. But he saw only the predator's shadow scurrying ahead.

"It might be leading us into a trap," Will said.

He knew Hook couldn't understand, yet he *felt* they were communicating.

Hook raised his snout defiantly, as if to say, *You want answers, let's go get them.*

Either the other predator had friends, or he knew his way around the caves and knew he could easily escape if any threat came too close.

If the latter were true, then the other predator just might know the way out.

Will and Hook followed the darting shadow. It led them down tunnels that Will had already explored, and across connecting ways he hadn't seen before.

Will marked the walls, desperately attempting to construct a full view of the maze in his mind.

The tunnels rose and fell, then Will had a sense that they were climbing higher than ever before. Hook was hobbling faster, as if he sensed Will's excitement.

The air became thinner. The darkness around them lifted slightly.

Will turned a corner and saw a beam of golden light streaking down from a tiny gap high above.

"Yes!" Will yelled.

Hook took a step back. He put one hand on Will's shoulder and tugged.

"What?"

Then Will heard it. A rumbling.

He scanned the small chamber into which their

quarry had led them and saw the slender dinosaur fully for the first time. It was pushing up against a cracked stone pillar, a single support that led to the roof ten feet above.

"No, wait!" Will called.

It was too late. With a grunt, the long-armed predator shoved at the pillar, then darted back as a section of the stone column cracked and fell away. The rumbling from above intensified, and stones dropped like bombs.

Will saw the small predator dart through the mouth of a tiny tunnel. It was quickly buried by debris as the ceiling continued to fall.

He turned and was nearly struck by a boulder that sealed the other entrance to the tunnel.

The flickering torch Will held fell, burning his hand on the way to the ground. He gasped as its light revealed another small gap low to the ground. He grabbed Hook and raced into the opening as the crashing at his back turned deafening.

The cave was sealed off in moments. Will scurried ahead, hearing Hook's labored breathing behind him.

Behind him...

Will drove himself on, praying the tunnel would widen out soon. It dipped suddenly, and he slid down twenty yards, yelping and growling, before he hit something hard with his head and came to a stop.

He was on the brink of passing out when he heard

Hook. The other raptor was above him, and if Hook chose to strike, Will could do nothing to defend himself.

He thought he heard Hook's sickle claw in the darkness.

A scratching came from the wall beside him. Three short marks.

Then silence.

Will's hands felt around until he could gather enough material to create another torch. He lit it and was surprised to see Hook resting nearby, watching him.

Craning his neck, Will saw the marks Hook had made on the wall.

They were crude imitations of the symbols Will himself had been making to keep track of their progress.

Will wasn't sure what to make of Hook's actions. Sometimes, he felt certain he understood the raptor.

Then again, back home he had thought he understood a lot of things that he really hadn't.

"Okay," Will said. He rose and held out a hand to Hook. "Let's try that again..."

CHAPTER 7

BOB

The search had gone badly. The branches Bob and the other Hippies had collected were either too big or heavy to move or too small to build a raft.

Finding good strong vines had not been a problem. Bob had set Leo and his buddies to that task while he tried to reason things out.

All the while, the Iguanodons—Spike, Sluggo, and Speed Racer—wandered along the shore. The huge dinosaurs glanced over now and then at all the noise the Hippies were making, but otherwise ignored them.

Without the guidance of their leader, the Hippies soon wandered from their task. Bob let them. He watched as curious Carl and imaginative Leo scurried down the shore to the Iggies.

Carl seemed content to stare at them from a safe distance. But Leo scrambled directly between Sluggo's feet and snatched a messy handful of greens from him!

Sluggo spun so quickly he nearly tripped, while the tail of the little Hypsilophodon whacked his backside. A roar sounded, and Sluggo swept at the air with his huge, heavy, spiked hand, raking and rending—

Nothing.

Leo was far too quick for the dinosaur.

Leo spat out the mouthful of greens and ran for cover in the forest. Sluggo stomped over, bent down, and ate them.

A few moments later, Leo and Carl were beside Bob. Carl looked intense. Leo was bounding in the air. Bob looked back to see Albert faking a limp and stumbling off to one side. Beside him, Hal hissed in fury and continued to gather vines and lay out the proper lengths.

Leo bounded toward the Iggies once more, and Bob called after him.

"Come on, they're not bothering you!"

The little Hypsilophodon was determined to be a nuisance. He sped around the trio of Iggies, annoying them until Spike and Sluggo both chased after him.

Sluggo slammed into a tree while trying to get at the smaller dinosaur, smashing branches to the ground.

Bob looked at the branches that had been dislodged.

They were just the right size!

Leo disappeared into the woods and the Iggies turned to Bob. Growling with frustration, they went back to their companion.

Bob went over to the fallen branches. They were just what he needed. Only—there weren't quite enough of them.

He looked to the Iggies near the water and shuddered. He knew what he had to do.

Bob motioned for Carl, Hal, and Albert to follow him. Leo ran after them.

I'll just act like I'm Will, Bob thought.

He went up on two legs and strutted as he approached the Iggies. He had to strain his neck to look up into their eyes.

Spike glared at him and growled low in his throat. A warning.

Please let me be as fast as I think I am, Bob thought as he took a deep breath, then *bit* Spike's flank.

The Iguanodon reared up and howled in surprise. The bite had been a tiny one and hadn't even broken the skin. But the act itself was one that couldn't be ignored.

Bob ducked as a sharp claw swept over his head, the wind and the hiss of the blow making him cry out in terror. Then he turned and ran, never looking back. The thundering, thudding footfalls of the Iguanodons were all he needed to hear.

Bob and the other Hippies led the Iguanodons down a winding trail between the trees closest to the shore. Bob leaped into branches, and so did his companions.

Spike, Sluggo, and Speed Racer, who weren't all *that* fast, smashed into the trees and raked heavy branches from their trunks.

Bob leaped from one branch to another, then dove to the ground. He scrambled beneath roots and leaped between the Iggies whenever possible, causing them to slam into each other as often as they did the trees.

Finally, when Bob was sure he had all the wood he needed, he turned to face the enraged dinosaurs. Leo and the other Hippies scampered behind him.

This is the really scary part, Bob thought.

He stood completely still as Spike and his pals drew up before him. Bob leaned down and held up a leafy branch as an offering.

Spike sniffed and came forward slowly, as if he expected more tricks.

Sounds came from behind Bob. Leo, looking to play some more.

Don't move, Bob thought, *willing* the other Hypsilophodon to calm down.

The shuffling from behind ceased.

Suspicion bright in his eyes, Spike reached down

and allowed Bob to feed the leaves to him. Spike chomped at them happily, grunting in pleasure.

Bob looked back to the other Hippies, who were already snapping off the leaf-bearing branches and making piles for the Iguanodons.

Sluggo and Speed Racer came forward and began eating, too.

Soon, everyone was happily getting along again. Spike even invited Bob to munch on a few of the greener leaves. Bob did it out of courtesy, but he had a lot more on his mind.

Bob put the Hippies to work. They dragged the heavy, stripped logs to the shore as Bob carefully tied the vines together.

He wished he could think of some way to rig up a sail, but he was going to have to settle for a paddle.

The work went on for the better part of two hours. Bob anxiously watched the woods, in case the Microvenators returned. He also worried that the Iguanodons would come over and mess with the raft Bob was assembling.

Their claws could tear it apart quite easily.

But there were no visitors, and the work went on. Bob tied knots the way he had been taught as a scout. He hoped that he had allowed the right amount of give, considering the vines would tighten once the raft was in the water.

He studied the deep, soft blue of the sky and was

relieved to see no trace of the storms that had plagued him since his arrival in the age of dinosaurs. There was a nice breeze, though, and it would be at his back as he traversed the lake, heading to Will and the others.

"Have I ever told you how much I loved adventure novels?" Bob asked Carl, who was taking a break. "I couldn't get enough of them when I was a boy. Robert Louis Stevenson. Jules Verne. Sir Walter Scott.

"Ah, and the illustrations, especially those by N. C. Wyeth...Just glorious. My family vacationed once in Chadds Ford, Pennsylvania, and they took me to the Brandywine River Museum, where I saw so many of the original paintings.

"I was never creative, but I could appreciate art. The paintings of young Arthur, the Black Arrow, *Treasure Island*..."

His tired muscles gained new strength, and his aches and pains were lifted as he relived those moments. He was midway through telling Carl a *Reader's Digest* version of *Treasure Island* when he looked down and realized that the raft was finished.

An unexpected sadness filled him as he looked to his companions. Their eyes were bright and expectant. They wanted to see what he had planned for them next.

But he had no plans. It was time for him to leave. Nothing he could say would make things any easier, so he simply turned his back on them, shoved the raft into the water, and leaped on board, gripping his oar. He had paddled a dozen feet out when he heard their cries. They ran along the shore, leaping, happily chasing after him.

He was about to wave good-bye when he saw movement from the woods. At first, he thought it was the Iggies.

Then a dozen speeding forms flew from cover.

The Microvenators.

Bob called to the Hippies, waving at them in warning.

They mimicked his movements, as if this were just another part of the game. Then the growls and hisses came, and they were louder than the creaks of the raft and the tiny splashes his creation caused as it tilted high on one side and came down hard on the other, like a seesaw.

Leo and the others sniffed the air and turned to face their attackers. Carl, who had earlier played the great swordsman, picked up one of the smaller branches and braced himself for the attack.

The others remained motionless.

Then Bob was yelling, "Get in the water! Swim to me! Hurry! Do it!"

But the Hippies didn't move.

Bob beat at the waters with his oar, a huge branch with a scooped-out, rounded knob at its base, and nearly fell into the water. His stomach lurched as the little raft rose and fell, threatening to upend itself at any moment.

Instants before the Microvenators could swarm the little plant-eaters, the Hypsilophodons turned, saw Bob's frantic motions, and plunged into the water.

"Yes!" Bob yelled. His enthusiasm faded as he closely studied the raft.

The branches were uneven, but the raft had a good four-by-eight feet of room on it. Just enough— barely—to fit all five of them. But could it take the strain?

He had no idea.

Leo and the other Hippies swam to the raft, and Bob hauled them on board.

The Microvenators were right behind them. Bob nearly fell as he swept at the water with his single oar, and the raft lifted so high that Carl and Hal almost slid into the water.

Then Carl revealed the branch that was still in his hand. Mimicking Bob's movements, he stood on the other side of the raft and beat at the waters with a frantic rhythm. The raft bobbed and headed forward, but it was not swift enough.

The first of the Microvenators came and grasped the edge of the raft. He was pulling himself on board, his teeth chattering hungrily, when Bob smacked him with his oar. The predator flew back, splashing into the water before two of his fellows.

The other Microvenators closed from either flank, swimming more quickly than Bob would have expected.

Their claws slashed at the raft, slicing at the vines holding the outer logs in place. Bob paddled harder, and a sudden breeze came up from behind, shoving at him like an invisible hand.

He struck at two more of the Microvenators, keeping the long-limbed predators from climbing aboard. But it felt hopeless. Soon, he or Carl would tire, or slip, and then—

Bob looked over to the other Hippies. They were close together now.

If they were just a little closer...

He yanked his companions together and kept them facing the wind, which was gaining power.

"Hold on!" he yelled, instinctively digging into the raft's wooden surface with his back claws. The other Hippies did the same, grabbing at each other, holding Bob on one side, Carl on the other. The wind struck them like a fist, but they held on.

As Bob stared in wonder, the raft got just enough speed to leave the Microvenators behind. Their bodies, pressed tight and anchored to the raft by their claws, had formed a sail!

Bob bellowed in triumph.

Sweeping at the water with his oar, he saw the group of Microvenators turn back toward shore.

"We did it!" Bob cried.

Then he felt it. A sense that had nothing to do with Bob London as a human being—*a primitive, animal fear.*

He turned and saw one of the Microvenators climbing up from behind him. The predator must have been clinging to the raft all along!

The predator surged onto the raft, making it shift and dip. Its mouth opened wide and its talon-like claws sprang out.

Mr. London shrank back.

He was dead. Done for. The final dinner bell had rung—and *he* was the featured entrée.

But there had to be a way out of this. *Something.*

Suddenly, images of battles at sea exploded in Mr. London's mind. Swashbuckling adventures. He lifted the branch he'd been using as an oar and waved it around like a pirate's sword.

The Microvenator shrieked in fury and attacked!

Bob shrank back, almost dropping his branch-oar.

Then Carl shoved ahead of him, striking the predator with the branch he carried. The Microvenator staggered back. Bob brought his branch up and stabbed with its blunt end, knocking the dinosaur back into the waters. It splashed down, slid beneath the raft.

Then the Microvenator emerged behind them,
spewing and spitting as it kept its head above water.
Bob and Carl went back to rowing, while the others
moved in tight once more, forming their sail.

The angry, struggling form of the Microvenator
dwindled as they sailed on.

Soon, it was gone completely.

Bob turned to Carl, Leo, Hal, and Albert. He set

three of them at different points on the raft to help maintain their balance, then rowed silently, proudly, with Carl toward the fiery call that Bob felt deep within him.

And for the first time in his life, Bob had something he'd never had before:

Friends.

CHAPTER 8

WILL

Will Reilly didn't think about his father very often. He sometimes laughed with his pals about his dad's preoccupation with business, or called his father Briefcase Man. He barely paid attention when his dad offered advice or bits of wisdom.

Yet now, as he moved down a long, dark corridor with Hook by his side, one of those lessons echoed in his mind: *Sometimes, not making a decision is making a decision.*

Will had found his way back to the main cave and hadn't run up against the long-armed predator again. It hadn't taken much time to check out the remaining tunnels. There was no hope of escape through any of them.

But Will *had* to escape. And right now he could think of only one way...

As he guided Hook around a corner, the familiar scent overwhelmed him—

MEAT-FOOD-PREY

—the heady aromas of life.

This was the end of the raptor pack's quest, the reason they'd come to the land above these caverns and camped there.

As Will led Hook to the large chamber that held the Tenontosaurus herd, he could feel the hunger, the *ache,* in his companion.

Suddenly, despite his wounded leg, Hook tried to leap ahead. But Will grabbed him back, steadying the raptor before he could fall.

A bellow rose from the darkness beyond.

Will tried to steel his uneasy nerves. The Tenontosaurs were not docile prey. He had to remind himself to be careful.

Will guided Hook into the large chamber. A glow from the wide, arcing ceiling lit the scene before them. Dozens of Tenontosaurs—old, young, strong, and weak—lay about the riverbanks.

Were they sleeping? Will wondered.

He needed to get past them to the underground river that flowed through this chamber. He intended to swim the narrow channel to wherever it might lead. Certainly, it would take him away from here—and with luck, it would lead him outside the mountain.

If the dinosaurs *were* sleeping, he could do it quietly, with no fear of a confrontation.

Unfortunately, Hook didn't share his view.

When the raptor realized the banquet that lay in front of him, Hook roared! Then he yipped and howled in delight.

Near the river, a handful of heavy, craggy heads rose.

Will tensed as the Tenontosaurs began to rise.

Hook roared again, then broke from Will, trying to leap toward them, despite his wounded leg. Will had to tackle the other raptor to the ground to stop him. Immediately, they began to wrestle.

Bringing Hook here had been foolish! Hook wouldn't be fast enough to avoid the many Tenontosaurs who were bound to attack, and his hunger was overriding his common sense— which should have been screaming for him to run away.

More of the Tenontosaurs were on their feet now. *I should have come here with a better plan,* Will realized. *I should have thought this through!*

Still struggling with Hook, Will managed to glance back to the tunnel. He had to haul Hook out of here and return when he'd figured all this out.

Only—

One of the Tenontosaurs had quickly, quietly circled behind them, cutting off their escape, while the other dinosaurs began to cry out in alarm. The animals' wails were deafening.

The noise! So much noise!

Will had to find another entrance to the cave system. Or he had to take Hook with him when he left the mountain by river, if possible.

That would surely mean Hook would lead the other raptors back here to the prey!

Will hesitated. He understood that there was a natural order to these things, but he didn't care. Tink had become his friend. And he didn't want to be the cause of getting her family ripped to shreds.

The Tenontosaurs trudged forward, moving like a line of soldiers advancing into battle. Will looked for some opening between them and thought that if he were on his own, he might be able to slip between them.

But he was on the ground now, still struggling with Hook, who wanted to do nothing more than to tear into the prey surrounding him.

Then an idea came to Will. He didn't like it, but it was the only thing he could think to do.

"I'm sorry," Will said.

Raising his foot, he kicked Hook hard in his wounded leg, nearly shattering the splint he had made for the dinosaur. Hook slumped forward, unconscious from the pain.

Will got to his feet and started dragging Hook. He scanned the walls of the vast cavern, looking for some other way in. Then he saw it—

An opening—on the other side of the river!

The Tenontosaurs closed on him. He hauled Hook up over his shoulder and ran. Two of the huge dinosaurs roared and followed. Others broke formation and hurried behind them.

Will revealed his sickle claws. As one of the Tenontosaurs swept its own heavy claw at him, Will spun and swept upward with his foot, slicing at the air in front of the dinosaur's nose.

With a yelp, the Tenontosaurus stumbled backward and crashed into another of its kind. They both fell.

They're weak, Will thought. *Their food source must be running out.*

But that didn't make them any less dangerous.

Another Tenontosaurus approached. Will attempted the same move on him, but Hook's weight threw him off and he fell, dumping the unconscious dinosaur to the ground.

Will saw a heavy foot descending and rolled swiftly. The foot slammed down next to Will's leg. It would have crushed his fragile bones.

"I'm *not* gonna eat you!" Will yelled, the words coming out in desperate yips. "I just want out of here!"

Several more thuds of heavy feet were his only answers.

Will scrambled toward Hook and grabbed him up again. Then, using the incredible muscles of his raptor body, Will leaped.

He flew over six feet and landed on a pile of stones. This time, Will held on to Hook and got his footing quickly. As the Tenontosaurs shifted, he saw a clear path to the river—

But what was he supposed to do with Hook?

The wounded Deinonychus couldn't swim with his injury. He wasn't even awake!

A shrill cry of pain sounded from Will's far left. The Tenontosaurs froze. Will scanned the dimly lit chamber and saw a young Tenontosaurus struggling with a small, long-armed dinosaur.

The predator was biting at the little plant-eater, darting in and away from the injured animal.

At least half the Tenontosaurs broke off their attack on Will and Hook and ran to the youth's defense.

Will immediately looked back toward the tunnel they'd come from. Had the long-armed predator entered the chamber that way?

No! The dinosaur guarding the entrance was still in place—

That meant the long-armed predator had found *another* way into this chamber on *this* side of the river!

Will heard Hook moan and felt the dinosaur start to twitch. He was waking up!

Will set Hook onto his one good leg and nodded

toward the little dinosaur under attack from the predator.

"Hey, look, it's our pal," Will whispered to Hook. "I bet you wouldn't mind a shot at him, would ya?"

Hook squealed and hissed. He hobbled toward the predator, ignoring the Tenontosaurs.

Will was about to follow when a heavy weight struck his back. Pain shot through him, and he fell to the ground. He rolled and saw a Tenontosaurus about to descend on him, claws at the ready.

"No!" Will yelled. Kicking out with his sickle claws, he struck the heavy muscle of the Tenontosaurus's thigh.

The dinosaur roared with fury and backed away long enough for Will to turn and get on his feet. He felt weaker now, and a tingling ran across his back.

He'd been wounded.

A volley of roars and screams came from his left. Will caught a glimpse of Hook scrambling through and beyond the group of Tenontosaurs. Hook followed the long-armed predator into a small cave Will hadn't seen before.

He turned and ran for the river. With a trio of Tenontosaurs chasing him, Will dove into the water.

It was freezing cold, and something on his back stung as he swam with the current. A weird smell came to him, along with a bitter taste he couldn't identify.

Several of the Tenontosaurs waded into the river, but they were too late.

Will swam furiously, his arms and legs kicking as he came to the far wall of the cave, took a deep breath, and dove below, praying he would be able to last until the river spilled outside once more.

CHAPTER 9

PATIENCE

The silence was getting on her nerves.

For the longest time, it had been Patience McCray's fondest wish that Zane McInerney would stop blathering. She had heard enough of his jokes to last a lifetime, and she had absolutely no interest in playing stupid games based on theme songs to old TV shows and movies.

But ever since they had faced the raptors on the shore, Zane had been moody and quiet. Even Runt had been unable to cheer him up.

In frustration, the baby dinosaur actually stopped following them. So Patience tied a collection of greens to Zane's tail to lure the little guy along.

She hoped that would get some comment out of the blubber-bellied long-neck.

It didn't. He simply endured the indignity, raising his tail when Patience told him to, lowering it so Runt could nibble when he was being a good little dinosaur.

Twilight was now approaching, and Patience could feel that knowing spot inside her growing warmer—the signal that they were approaching Ground Zero.

She noticed the land around them had changed. The hills had become mountains as they continued their movement through a rust-colored valley. Amber, crimson, and violet streaked the sky.

Patience decided that in the interest of hearing another human voice in her head, she was willing to make the ultimate sacrifice:

"Listen," she told Zane, "I'm ready for more of those girly-girl lessons, if you want."

Zane was silent. His huge camel-like lips seemed to be set in a pout. Or a scowl.

Patience gave up. She sniffed and scented prey just ahead. Something she could scavenge.

She broke from the brontos and approached a mud flat that ran into the base of a mountain. Her feet *splooshed* in the muck as she waded in. She could see the tracks of several creatures that had passed just ahead. Though she didn't like her meals this way, she was hungry enough not to care.

She was in the muck up to her thighs when she felt it starting to pull her down.

Panic gripped her, just as her hunger began to flood her brain with a feverish desire to move forward, to seize the food just ahead at any cost, and—

Thhhhhhh-wackkkkkkkk!

The sound made her jump! Patience turned and saw Zane tapping his tail on the ground.

"Back out slowly," Zane said. "It's called a predator trap. One animal gets stuck in the deep mud and can't get out. Its scent and its calls draw a predator. That one goes in and can't get out. Then another one goes in and another and so on and so forth.

"Big bodies, tiny brains. That's a dinosaur for ya."

Patience backed out of the mud, her hunger under control.

"Thanks," she said, brushing at the muck covering the lower half of her body. Her stomach growled. She was still hungry.

"Whatever," Zane said. He headed off, with Runt trailing behind him, nibbling on the leaves tied to his tail.

Patience's eyes narrowed. She could no longer hide her irritation.

"*What* is your *problem?*" she asked.

"I don't have a problem," Zane said. "Except that we're going off to Ground Zero, where we're probably going to get eaten or whatever. Other than that, I'm fine."

"No, you're *not,*" Patience said.

"Hey, come on. You forget. I'm Zane *no* brain. Or, if you prefer, I'm actually more like the dinos. Brain the size of a pea." He tapped his head on a nearby rock. "Not much up there. So how could there be anything on my mind?"

"That's something else," Patience said. Her stomach growled again, but she ignored it. "Why are you always acting like you're not that bright when you are?"

He snorted. "Yeah. I'm a real brain trust."

"I'm beginning to think you are," Patience said. "Way more than you let on."

Zane's head bobbed on its long neck. "Like you care."

The words stung. Patience had been telling him—and herself—that she didn't really care. But for some reason, Zane's mood was important to her.

"I saved your butt," she said. "You owe me."

Zane stopped, nostrils flaring. "Schrödinger's Cat."

"Pardon?"

"It's a scientific principle about stasis. About things not changing."

Patience waited. She wasn't following.

He raised his chin. "You want to hear this?"

Weirdly enough, she did. At least, they were talking again.

"The idea is, you take a cat and you put him in a box with two possible food supplies. One is poisoned, the other isn't. Then—"

Patience whacked her tail on the ground. "I like cats."

"Well, this isn't a real experiment. It's theoretical. A real scientific principle, what some call the mascot of new physics. A guy named Erwin Schrödinger came up with it. But, see, the thing is, no one ever really put a cat in a box and—"

"I have cats."

Zane sighed. "What about gerbils?"

"Don't like gerbils. Not a gerbil kind of person."

"Okay. So it's a gerbil. 'Schrödinger's Gerbil,' all right?"

"And it's in this box," Patience said. "It's either going to eat the good food or the bad."

"Well, it's going to be fed one or the other, based on the random decay of a radioactive sample. Something that can't be predicted and can't be quantified from the outside."

"So you do—what? Wait?"

"Yeah. That's exactly it. The box is secure. The gerbil can't escape."

"This is creepy."

"There's a point."

"Imagine *my* relief," Patience said.

"According to the experiment, one can leave the box alone and so long as one never opens it, the gerbil inside is in what's called an indefinite state. It's neither alive nor dead."

"How much food are we talking about here? I mean, after a while, is it going to be, 'Gee, it's not making any more gerbil noises'?"

"The point is that while it makes sense that the gerbil would now be an ex-gerbil—"

Patience giggled. She couldn't help herself. "An ex-gerbil. I like that."

"Thank you. The bottom line is that until you open the box and check, you really don't know for sure. Theoretically speaking."

"And the gerbil thing relates to why you're in such a lousy mood—how?"

"Things don't change. People don't change." Zane looked away. "You won't change. You're just like the gerbil."

"Excuse me?"

"I mean it. You're doing this whole tomboy thing, picking fights like it's still fifth grade, doing everything you can not to grow up...you're like everything else. Trapped in stasis. Unwilling or unable to change."

Patience felt her anger rise. "You think you have some idea of what things are like for me?"

Zane shook his head. "No. I don't. And that means that you don't have the first real clue about me, either."

She stepped back, stunned.

He was right.

Zane started walking again. "Everyone looks at me and is like, oh, it's the funny, fat kid. Okay, we get that. We can deal with that. But the *smart*, funny, fat kid? No way. That wouldn't fly. Too much information. Too much nonconformity with standards and expectations. Just not gonna happen. At least with people thinking they get what I'm all about—"

"There's something else," Patience said. She didn't know why she said it. A feeling, maybe.

Zane stopped. "It doesn't matter."

"Oh, right. You lay all this on me. You tell me what all my problems are, but—"

"Hey!" a voice called.

Patience stiffened as she smelled a new scent in the air. A predator.

Another raptor.

She looked to the right. A single raptor stood on the cliff overlooking their valley.

"Are you two gonna break it up or do I have to get Mr. London to send you to the principal's office?"

Patience couldn't believe it. *That voice!* It was—

"Will!" Zane shouted.

They stared at their fellow classmate, now in the body of a ferocious-looking raptor. Patience was about to speak when stones suddenly fell from the opposite cliff.

Patience turned her head to see five Hypsilophodons staring down at them.

"Glad to see things haven't been dull," Mr. London called. "Now, how about we get together and see if we can figure out how to get home?"

"Well, whattaya know," Zane said to Patience, the heaviness finally gone from his tone. "The gang's all here."

CHAPTER 10

WILL

Night fell.

Will found food a few miles off, near the edge of the vast lake where Mr. London had docked. Then he called for Patience to join him for dinner.

She said very little. He guessed that the hunger probably had a pretty firm hold on her, and he figured she was probably more than a little embarrassed over having to feed in front of someone else. Will certainly was.

Still, he had a feeling that there was something she wanted to say to him. Her maw opened wide—and she silently trawled for fish.

They returned in silence and sat with the others around a campfire. Mr. London's Hypsilophodon friends were hesitant to come anywhere near a raptor at first, and Runt had made threatening, defensive gestures, but eventually everyone settled in.

Mr. London pointed to Will. "So—tell us everything."

Will filled him in on what he had pieced together about the big event due tomorrow.

The Hippie gang nodded gravely.

"So the raptors came to Ground Zero hunting the Tenontosaurs?" Mr. London asked.

"Yes," said Will. "Seems to me the herd went inside the mountain hoping to throw off the hunters. There must have been an earthquake that trapped them inside."

One of the little Hippies slowly approached Will.

"That's Carl," Mr. London said. "Don't mind him, he's just curious."

Carl came within a foot of Will, sniffed, and leaped back, his features scrunched up, as if he had just taken a whiff of something really gross.

He rejoined his friends.

"They're not very polite, I know," Mr. London said. He sounded more amused than apologetic.

Patience sniffed, too. So did Zane.

"Guys, you're giving me a complex," Will said. He laughed and smelled his underarms. "Come on, already! I can't smell *that* bad!"

Zane's camel lips scrunched up in what looked like distaste. "Actually, you smell like you just stopped at the local quick mart to gas up."

Mr. London laughed, and the other Hippies made similar noises.

Everyone stared at the teacher.

"What?" Mr. London asked. "It was funny!"

Will looked away. Mr. London had certainly loosened up. And the way the Hippies followed him around, acting like his buds, was *weird*.

Then there was this thing about how he smelled—

Will touched his snout with one hand. But he couldn't smell much at all. Now that he thought about it, ever since he'd climbed out of the river, his scent ability had been numbed. That was weird, too.

"Well," Will said with a shrug, "I do remember smelling something in the water. Something kind of strange."

"Tell us the rest of what happened," Mr. London said. "Don't leave anything out."

"Yeah, entertain and inform," Zane said.

Will was surprised by Zane's tone. His friend sounded almost nasty. He'd seen Zane grouse before, but this was different.

Will recounted his adventures with the raptor pack, doing his best to make it seem that he was just trying to get close to the Big Guy in order to find out more about Ground Zero. That was what he had told himself at the time. Now he was no longer so sure.

"Then they dumped me in the mountain," Will said. He spoke of his meeting with Tink and of his explorations of the tunnels.

When he came to the part about the long-armed predator knocking the torch from his hand near the gas-filled chamber, Mr. London stopped him.

"That was a Microvenator," Mr. London said. "We had to fight off a whole bunch of them!"

And suddenly, Will's teacher was talking about his own adventures, as if he were trying to one-up Will.

The small-bodied science teacher was halfway through his swashbuckling tale when Zane interrupted.

"So, Will," Zane began, "are you saying there was a gas cap down there?"

Mr. London raised his chin and bulged his eyes. He looked like he was on the verge of pouting. "I was talking!"

Will ignored Mr. London and answered Zane. "I guess so. I got woozy walking from one end to the other. And I could hear a kind of hissing from this one spot on the floor."

Zane nodded. "So there are natural-gas deposits in the mountain. Probably crude oil, too. Like what's in the river, and what makes you stink so bad."

Mr. London's head wobbled from side to side and his eyes rolled. He made little *yeah-yeah-yeah-talk-talk-talk-blah-blah-blah* motions with his right claw.

The four other Hippies mimicked his movements.

"This is important!" Zane said.

"Yeah, right," Mr. London muttered. "Who died and left you brains?"

Patience gasped. She rose and roared at the teacher. "What's gotten into you?"

"Hey, I've got every right to an opinion," Mr. London said. He sounded childish.

The situation had gone from weird to *very* weird.

Will looked over. Zane's eyes were burning. He said nothing as Runt quietly stole behind the teacher and let out a burp that made the Hypsilophodon leap into the air and scramble away from the fire, his friends dutifully following.

Oh, man, Will thought. *Is that what it looked like back home? Me and my buds, my pack, with them doing whatever I did, whatever I said?*

A sudden rumbling captured everyone's attention. Will looked up to the walls of the valley on either side of them.

The ground shook suddenly, and a roar sounded from the darkness!

"Look out for rocks!" Will said. He leaped to his feet, worried he was about to be caught in another rock slide.

The tremors subsided quickly. The earth stopped rolling. The minor quake was at an end.

"Seismic disturbances," Mr. London said. He was trembling, and he was using his teacher voice again. "Very common."

Another noise rose in the night. A low and very localized rumble that sounded different from the sounds that came from the quake.

"I'm gonna check out that sound," Patience said. She sounded uneasy. "You guys wait here."

She lumbered into the darkness.

Mr. London started pacing. He circled the flames. "I think I have an idea of what Ground Zero is all about. But if I'm right, no one's—"

"We've been thinking of it as Ground Zero for a reason," Zane said, cutting him off.

Mr. London froze. He stared at the long-neck incredulously. "Yes."

The long-neck bobbed his head. His gaze was narrow with concentration. "There are natural-gas reserves built up under enormous pressure beneath the mountain. Combine that with crude oil, lots of flint, and some other combustibles. A few rocks hitting each other the right way, a few sparks in the right places, and it all goes up. One big explosion."

"Ground Zero," Will whispered in horror, thinking of the trapped Tenontosaurs, of Hook, and of the pack that would be bombarded by stones flying like shrapnel.

Mr. London nodded.

"So how do we stop it?" Zane asked. "If that's it, if that's what we were sent here to do, then how do we pull it off?"

"I don't think we can," Mr. London said.

Will rose up suddenly, angry and frustrated. "I don't accept that."

Mr. London became childish again. "Fine, well, I guess that settles things, huh? I couldn't possibly be right if the great Will Reilly disagrees."

"What is your problem?" Will asked.

"You," Mr. London said. "You're everyone's problem."

Will stalked closer to the teacher. "What did you just say?"

"I turned on the machine," Mr. London said. "I'll own up to that. But I wasn't the one with *issues* that needed to be worked out."

I wouldn't be so sure, Will thought. But he kept silent. He wanted to hear this.

Zane looked over in warning. "We don't know anything for sure, Mr. L. Stop it."

The teacher-turned-little-Hippie stood and raised his snout defiantly. "The M.I.N.D. Machine needed something to focus on. Some*one* who needed all of this, for whatever reason."

Will was stunned. "You're saying this is all my fault?"

"You lost the election. You wanted to create a situation in which you could be the hero again, in which everyone would be looking at you like you were *all that*." Mr. London shook his head.

"That's what Patience and Zane said."

Will's shoulders slumped. What Mr. London said was true. He had wanted all that and more.

And he'd wanted to get away from Wetherford. As far away as possible...

"Then there are those games you like playing," Mr. London said. "The video games, where you triumph against the impossible—"

"All right!" Will said. "Whatever. Even if you're right, it doesn't change anything."

Silence stretched across the campsite. Then footsteps came.

Two sets of footsteps.

"I don't believe there's no way of keeping Ground Zero from happening," Patience said from the darkness. There was a shape beside her. One almost as big as her. "And I don't think any of you really believe it, either."

Zane stepped back as the shape beside Patience was lit by the flames. It was another Acrocanthosaurus—a sailback, like her.

"Whoa!" Zane hollered. "That's the one that tried to *eat* me!"

Will instantly leaped to protect his friend. "Stay back!" he told Zane. "I'll make sure that thing doesn't hurt you!"

Zane's plant-eater snout whacked Will from behind, knocking him over.

"What was that for?" Will snarled. He looked back at the long-neck and his little brother. Both were glaring.

"Cut it out," Patience said. "This is G.K. He's a friend." Her teeth gleamed in the firelight in what might have been a smile. "And he just gave me an idea."

CHAPTER 11

PATIENCE

The group didn't have far to travel, and they all needed sleep. Patience volunteered to take first watch, but her fatigue quickly caught up with her. She watched G.K. settle into a deep slumber and quickly found herself doing the same.

Patience was awakened by tiny pressures against her flank. She heard chirps, squeals of delight, then felt a slightly harder pressure against her leg.

Opening one eye, she saw Mr. London and four of his little Hippie friends gathered near her. Mr. London poked at her scales with one finger, then urged his new friends to do the same.

"This Acrocanthosaurus is a fine example of a mid-Cretaceous predator, don't you think?" Mr. London asked. "While the top running speed of a Deinonychus, or *raptor*, exceeds that of the Acrocanthosaurus, this animal can move quite quickly, and with a much, much greater stride. In a footrace, they might be evenly matched. The

Deinonychus, however, has the greater agility and can turn in midstride with practically the speed of thought.

"So in an obstacle course, or, say, an extreme sporting event, you'd probably want to wager on the Deinonychus, whereas in a contest of brute strength and cunning, the Acrocanthosaurus will be the winner."

Patience closed her eye and pretended to sleep. The hardest part was not cracking up. She knew that if she laughed, the diminutive dinosaurs wouldn't hear human giggles. They would hear a gigantic predator growl and *snorf*, rumble, and cough.

She didn't want to scare them. But Mr. L was talking like a museum curator! Or like he was back in a classroom. It was terrifyingly adorable. Not that she'd let him know that.

One of the Hippies strolled over to G.K.

Patience watched, certain that her fellow Acro was asleep. Suddenly, G.K. sprang, grasping the smaller dinosaur in his hands, his maw open wide to take a nice big bite!

Patience roared and G.K. hesitated, looking at her curiously. She nodded at the Hippie and motioned for G.K. to drop him.

He did.

The shivering Hypsilophodons scurried to Mr. London, who stood in front of the rest of his friends.

"What do you want, anyway?" Patience yelled at G.K. "Why do you keep following me?"

The sailback stared at her, his gaze narrowing.

He walked away without a sound.

Patience lay on her side, watching him in the pale moonlight until he had walked a thousand feet and stopped, his face turned toward the stars.

Mr. London sat beside her. His friends were a dozen yards back, huddled around the one who had almost been eaten.

"Thanks," he said softly. "I really hadn't thought—"

"No, I guess not."

Mr. London picked at his teeth, freeing a little chunk of greens. "Do you want to talk about what's going on with you and G.K.?"

"Not with *you*."

Mr. London flinched, as if her words had stung.

"Sorry," she said. "It's complicated."

"I'll leave you to it, then." Mr. London turned and slowly walked away. He stopped and looked back three times, as if he was expecting her to call him back.

She didn't.

Sighing, he ambled back to her anyway.

"What?" she asked, truly annoyed. Then she noticed that he was shaking. "Are you cold?"

He looked away, glancing at his friends. It came

to her suddenly: he was worried about them. About *all* of them, not just his Hippie friends.

So why was he coming to her? She had her own problems to deal with.

"Zane told me about the girly-girl lessons," Mr. London said. "I could help."

"Uh-huh."

"Do you know how to dance?"

Patience snorted. "Why? Do you want to teach me?"

Mr. London nodded. "If you're going to Will's party, and you really want that witch Monique to buy into your act, you're going to need more than a makeover and a pretty dress."

"Right," Patience said. She was no longer certain that she was going to Will's party. So much had happened during her time here. Seeing her family, for one—

No—her *host's* family, this Acro's family. She *had* to remember that.

"Take my hands," Mr. London said. He stood on his back legs, hands outstretched.

Patience stood. This was ridiculous.

She took his hands anyway, hauling him up roughly.

"Gently," he said, dangling in the air. "Gently."

"Whatever."

"Now think of music. Something slow."

A rustling came from behind them. Will and Zane appeared—and music filled the night. Zane was using his powers again. Runt trotted up beside him.

"I didn't know you could do that," Will said.

"Shut up," Zane said. "You'll break my concentration."

Patience felt uncomfortable enough to start with. Having an audience was only making it worse.

"There will always be other people around when you have a party," Mr. London said. "That's kind of the point."

She closed her eyes and listened to Mr. London's instructions. Soon she was moving in time to the music, performing the steps he taught her.

Looking down at his dangling little body, his feet almost touching hers, she was reminded of the way a parent teaches a child to dance. For some reason, the thought made her happy.

"Can I cut in?" Will asked.

"No," Patience and Mr. London said in unison. They looked at each other and laughed.

The music soon faded, and Patience allowed Mr. London to drop to the ground. Patience gave a slight bow and turned to see G.K. staring at her.

She went to him and nuzzled his cheek.

Then they settled down next to each other and silently stared at the stars.

PART TWO
PLEUROCOELUS
PARADOX

CHAPTER 12

ZANE

Zane was dreaming about being back home, in his own body, his own bed. Suddenly, an alarm clock sounded. He rolled over and tried to pull a pillow over his head to block out the sound. Only—he wasn't in bed, and there were no pillows.

"Make it stop!" Patience yelled. Her Acro boyfriend growled beside her.

Zane shook himself awake and the noise faded. He blinked a few times and found Mr. London standing in front of him.

"You have to be able to control your imaginative power," the Hypsilophodon lectured. "Everything's riding on it!"

"Yeah, I know, I know..." Zane's long neck ached. Next to him, Runt sneezed.

The group pulled together, found food, and headed for Ground Zero. They took a route Will had chosen in order to keep their scents hidden from the raptor pack in the valley.

They walked together through valleys, around rock slides, over small rises, and toward a long stretch of beautiful mountains a mile ahead.

Zane didn't bother to ask if they were there yet. Mr. London had gotten annoyed the last eight times he'd done it, and besides, he'd felt the same general warmth from his connection to this place for some time.

The biggest excitement of the morning had been the armadillo crossing. Of course, Mr. London had said they weren't armadillos at all. They were Nodosaurus, little fellas who belonged to the same family as spike-backed Ankylosaurus.

Zane knew that, of course. But he didn't bother saying anything. Besides, they still looked like armadillos to him. And they crossed a well-traveled road that might have been a dinosaur highway, so it struck him as kind of funny.

"Just ahead," Mr. London said. "Slow down."

Patience frowned. "What? You've gotta go do your business or something?"

"Knock it off," Will said. "We're here."

"Do you treat your teammates on the basketball court like this?" Mr. London asked Patience.

Patience seemed oblivious to Mr. London's critical tone. She tilted her head and lifted her snout before casually answering, "Yes."

He turned his little pink and green beak away.

"Why am I not surprised?"

Zane got between them. Somewhere in the hilly ground ahead, on one of the gentle slopes or behind one of the sharp reddish rises and flattop ranges, the future waited.

He, for one, was terrified.

"Maybe this isn't such a good idea," Zane said.

"You can't back out," Patience said. "We're all here for a reason. It's gonna take all of us if we're gonna get back."

Will came up to him. "Listen. Mr. L and me, we're the ones who are going in. You'll have Patience and G.K. and Runt to protect you. It'll be—"

"*Fine,*" Zane said, suddenly furious.

The raptor threw up his hands. "I have no idea what this is all about."

"Clearly."

"I thought we were friends."

Zane looked away. "That doesn't excuse every-thing."

Mr. London motioned to Will. "Come on. We don't know how long we've got."

"We'll talk about this back home," Will promised.

Sure we will, Zane thought. He knew about Will's promises. Good intentions and all that. *Jerk.*

Mr. London held up the amber key. "We still don't know what this is for."

Zane nodded. "It could be for just about anything. Amber has electrical properties—the Romans and the Greeks figured that out. And it's used to heal, 'cause it's got succinic acid in it.

"Actually, people have been using amber for centuries to treat asthma, rheumatism, aching joints, pneumonia, insect bites, whatever. Dinosaurs get sick, too."

Will and Mr. London gaped at Zane.

Funny, thought Zane, when he was using his brain, the fear left him.

"I remember the things I read," Zane said simply. "Get over it."

"I'm cool," Will said.

Mr. London shook his head. "Definitely." He drew a sharp breath. "I think I should take it with me. I don't know why. Just a feeling."

Zane had no problem with that. Neither did Patience or Will.

"See you, then," Mr. London said.

"Good luck, guys," Will added.

The pair turned and walked off. Zane watched as the four Hypsilophodons scurried after Mr. London. The teacher kept shooing them, telling them to stay behind, but they stayed at his side.

Suddenly Patience called out to Will. He stopped and waited as she ran to him. Zane cocked an ear to eavesdrop.

"Listen," she told Will, "about what happened in

the lunchroom. My, y'know, punching your lights out."

"I remember."

"Yeah, well, about that..."

Zane couldn't believe what he was witnessing. Patience McCray was about to make an apology. So far as he knew, she had never apologized for anything in her life!

Zane looked over at G.K. "Exactly what did you *do* to her when you guys were together, anyway?"

G.K. looked away imperiously.

Zane turned his attention back to Will and Patience.

She must not realize I can hear her, Zane mused.

He thought about saying something, but his instincts told him that if he interrupted this moment, Patience would never say what she was about to say. And he felt that she needed for this moment to happen.

"Here's the thing," Patience said. "Last year. That guy Marcus. The one who got hurt during track, pole-vaulting. The mat wasn't where it should have been. He ended up in a wheelchair."

"Yeah," Will said. He looked confused. "I helped out in the fund-raisers—"

"I know. Marcus and me, we were best buds. The first person I ever really trusted after my friend Carol-Anne set off a fire in the orphanage when we were kids, then blamed me. Or since the woman who adopted me got sick and couldn't do anything when her relatives had me put in that place and wouldn't let me see her or talk to her.

"That's why I ran away from there, to try and see her. You've probably heard these stories. Parts of them."

Will stared into her eyes. He waited.

"Marcus wanted me to come to the hospital. I didn't go. His parents begged me to come see him in rehab. I said I would and I didn't. They moved when they started that lawsuit against the school and Marcus called a hundred times, but I never called him back, never wrote him, never did anything. I knew I was wrong, but I was stuck somehow. Frozen.

"I felt like he had just gone away on me."

She looked over to G.K., then turned her gaze back on Will. "Not everybody goes away. I mean, I know that now. I learned it here. So I guess it wsn't all so bad, coming here. I just wanted you to know that."

"All right," Will said. "I mean...thanks."

Zane had to force himself to shut his gaping mouth and pretend he hadn't been able to hear any of that. Patience moved to his side.

It hadn't been an apology. Not exactly. But it was something. A gesture of friendship. And a real step for her. Zane was impressed, though he did his best not to show it.

"Still scared?" Patience asked Zane.

"Oh, yeah."

"Then do me a favor," she said. "Tell me about the gerbil one more time. I'm not sure I get it."

Zane didn't take his gaze off the departing members of their team. There was every chance that the mountain could explode when they were in it.

But the plan they had agreed upon was their only chance of getting home.

He wished he hadn't been so hard on Will.

"Uh, Zane?" Patience asked. "Hello?"

"One gerbil, locked in a box," he said mechanically. "A vial of poison gas and some radioactive atoms for company. Until the box is opened, the gerbil's got a fifty-fifty chance. You can cling to hope.

"Once it *is* opened, you just have to go with what you're left. Welcome to quantum physics. That'll be five dollars, please."

Patience touched his flank. "We just opened the box, didn't we?"

He looked at her, then nodded. "Yeah. If we decided not to do this, if we said, let's just stay here and play it safe, let's not worry about anyone's future but ours, we'd always be wondering. We'd live our lives in an indefinite state. Would it have worked? What would have happened?"

He considered how much more frightening that would be than actually facing the future.

CHAPTER 13

WILL

Will noticed the way Mr. London kept his distance as they walked to the river that led into the mountain's underground passages.

At first, Will thought it was because the other Hippies were afraid of him. He could understand that, though he didn't like it much. Then he kept going over what Mr. London had said last night.

"So, what's the matter?" Will finally asked. "Do you really think this is all my fault? That it all comes down to the M.I.N.D. Machine trying to give me what it thought I wanted?"

Mr. London didn't even look his way.

That was as much of an answer as Will needed.

They reached the river in silence. Will had already described the swim they would be facing.

"This isn't what I wanted," Will said as he stood on the river's edge. "Not even close."

He dove in.

The water was icy, despite the bright sunlight

pouring down from above. He swam against the current, and the solid wall of the mountainside was right in front of him. He dove below, and the water became murky.

By the time he reached the pure darkness that meant he was beneath the mountain, Will felt as if his lungs might explode. He looked back and saw Mr. London and the other Hippies swimming behind him.

One of the Hippies looked weak, as if he wasn't going to make it. Mr. London grabbed his hand and pulled him forward.

Will saw a dull greenish light above and swam for the surface. He burst from the water, gasping for air, and narrowly avoided the swipe of a Tenontosaurus's claw!

"Hold on!" Will screamed. "Just let us—"

The five Hypsilophodons broke through the surface behind him. Will saw that a half-dozen large Tenontosaurs were gathered on the bank before him. They looked away from him, distracted by the sight of Mr. London and the other plant-eaters.

"Blahhhhhhhh!" Mr. London hollered, waving his arms. "Wahhhhh-hooooooo!"

The other Hippies made funny faces and imitated the odd sounds that came from Mr. London. The Tenontosaurs stared at them in surprise.

Will took advantage of the distraction. He swam fifty feet beyond the gathering of Tenontosaurs and scrambled onto the bank.

No guards stood near the tunnel mouths. Will raced toward the entrance he knew best and paused to look back and make sure Mr. London saw where he was heading.

The Hippie gave a kind of thumbs-up amid his clowning around. Will raced into the tunnel and soon found himself climbing up and away from the main cavern. He couldn't see a thing, but he had the route memorized.

He dried himself off by rolling around on the dirty floor of the tunnel, waited where he told Mr. London he would wait, and spent his time using roots and vines to make two torches, one for each of them. He had just finished when Mr. London and his soaking wet friends appeared.

"Wipe your feet," Will said. "You'll get mud everywhere."

Mr. London dried himself off as Will lit one of the torches. He handed it to the teacher.

There was no need for further discussion. The tension between them hadn't eased.

Nor had the danger they were sharing.

Will led Mr. London to the collection of eggshell fragments he had discovered in one of the lower chambers, and together they set to work.

Will and Mr. London put a dozen of the broken shells back together, wrapping them with wet leaves and vines to keep them from falling apart. Then they filled the shell "bowls" with deposits of crude oil that leaked from the walls in other caverns.

They handed shells to Carl and the rest of the Hippies to be carried back to the Tenontosaurus cavern.

Bombs, that's what they'd made. Patience's idea. When she had come back with the other sailback, she said simply, "We're idiots. Everything we need is already right in front of us."

She had gone on to describe the plan that had come to her, and it was a very good plan, everyone had to admit.

The only thing that hadn't been entirely clear was why the return of her suitor, G.K., had prompted it.

That was a mystery for another time. Their true time. If they could just get back to it.

Will could feel the presence of the raptors on the other side of the mountain. He was well aware that if the raptors knew there was more prey so very close, they would come running. There would be no arguing with them. No reasoning. They were wild, hungry—

HUNGRY-HUNGRY-HUNGRY

—and desperate.

A part of him still wanted to be with them.

Once the bombs, or "boomers" as Zane called them, were ready, Will stood off to the side. Mr. London took his torch. Huge lengths of dry vine were rolled around the beak-faced teacher's shoulder and arm.

"Good luck," Mr. London said, not looking at Will.

"You too," Will said.

He watched Mr. London lead his troops away, their light quickly fading. He was well aware of what he was supposed to do now: nothing. Just *wait*.

But there was something that hadn't been accounted for in Patience's plans.

No—some*one*.

Will bent down and lit the other torch. Then he turned and trotted off, in search of Hook.

CHAPTER 14

BOB

Bob London led Carl and the other Hippies back to the cave of the Tenontosaurs.

The torch he held drew the attention of several of the lumbering dinosaurs, but that was all. His fellow plant-eaters made no move to stop him as he handed his torch to Carl and got to work.

The amber key was tied to his waist with a piece of vine. Zane had been right—there were many possible uses for the key.

Why hadn't any of that occurred to him? He was a teacher. A scientist. Yet he was acting like a thirteen-year-old.

And he *felt* like a thirteen-year-old.

As he climbed along the ledges lining the cavern's back wall, planting the bombs as he went, Bob wondered why he'd been acting so cruel to Zane and especially to Will. It wasn't like him at all.

He thought of the story he had told the Hypsilophodons:

There once was a boy who had found a golden key...

Bob looked at the amber key dangling from his vine belt.

He drew a sharp breath and found Albert curiously staring at him.

"It doesn't mean anything," Bob whispered. "I just thought of the story because we found the key. It's not like Bertram's M.I.N.D. Machine put the key here because I used to love that story."

Albert cocked his head, as if weighing those thoughts.

Suddenly angered, Bob grabbed at the collection of explosive boomers Albert carried.

"What d'you know," Bob snapped. He grabbed one of the boomers and looked over the ledge, a dozen feet down. "Carl, I can't see. Throw me that thing!"

Carl didn't get it at first. Bob pointed at the torch, made throwing motions, and Carl happily obliged.

Only—he missed.

The torch landed ten feet back, next to one of the strategically placed boomers. With a hiss, it struck the vine fuse that Bob had set into it.

"No...," Bob whispered.

The explosion knocked Bob and the three other Hippies from the ledge. A brilliant light flared yellow and white as a terrible thunder sounded and a rain of stones fell on the other dinos.

A moment later, Bob found himself on the ground, aching, sore, and panicked. What if Patience and Zane heard that explosion and thought that was the signal they were waiting for?

He heard a chorus of angry, curious *groomphs* and *glorphs*. Glancing up, he saw that a group of Tenontosaurs was staring down at him.

"Everyone stay calm," Bob urged.

Two of the Tenontosaurs roared. One lunged forward and grabbed Bob, lifting him high into the air. He felt the vine that held the amber key in place loosening, the key about to fall.

Suddenly, Bob had only one urge. He grasped the key and held it away from him as far as he could. He didn't want anything happening to the key. For some reason, making sure it was all right meant more to him now than even protecting the future!

He felt a strange warmth at his back and saw the Tenontosarus's expression change. The anger faded. The dinosaur appeared transfixed.

Bob looked over his shoulder. A single beam of bright amber light was shining down from the hole that had been blown by the boomer. It struck the amber key, and beautiful prism-like shards of multicolored kaleidoscopic light shot forward in every direction.

Slowly, the Tenontosaurus set him down. Bob

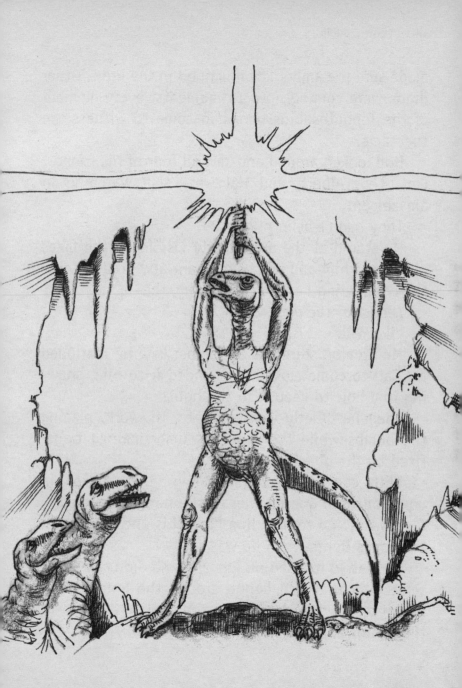

made sure the amber key remained in the light. Other dinos were coming now. In moments, every member of the Tenontosaurus herd had come to witness the spectacle.

Bob looked around and saw all four of his friends. Carl, Leo, Albert, and Hal were also watching in amazement.

They hadn't been hurt!

He stared at the awe clearly visible on the faces all around him and felt triumphant and bold. He was the conquering hero, the cool guy, the—

Leader of the pack.

Like Will.

Mr. London stared at the amber key. He motioned for Carl to come closer and handed it to him, showing him how to keep it in the light.

Then he quietly went back to his work, placing the bombs while the Tenontosaurs remained transfixed by the glowing key.

With care, Mr. London strung vines soaked in crude oil from one boomer to the next. This lengthy fuse was going to help him blow this entire string of Christmas lights when he was ready.

He was so focused on his work, he didn't hear the scratching that had begun around the hole he had blown to the outside—or the tiny yips of excitement that followed.

CHAPTER 15

PATIENCE

"Look," Patience whispered to Zane.

Raptors were climbing the mountain. Three small predators. Juveniles.

Zane shuddered. "They were probably off playing. That's why they're not with the pack."

Patience watched them dig at the edges of the tiny hole created by the explosion inside the mountain. It wouldn't take long before they made it big enough for one of them to slip through.

"What do we do now?" Zane asked. He sounded scared again. "They're not going back to get the others. There're just three of them, and they're pretty small. If I mojo up some more Iggies or something to try and lead them away, they might just run off and get their buddies, their parents, whoever."

Patience saw his point. An illusion of Iguanodons wasn't going to be their way out this time.

Right now, the raptors were contained. There was every chance that Mr. London and Will would be able to blow an opening in the side of the mountain large enough for the Tenontosaurs to escape long before these guys could get in.

But there was also the question of why one of the bombs had gone off sooner than it was supposed to.

Was Mr. London all right? What about Will?

Then she saw it. Streaks of multicolored light bursting from the tiny opening.

The little raptors sat back, staring at the light. They took playful swipes at it, then settled down, content to just watch it shimmer.

"They're all right," Patience whispered. "Don't ask me how I know. I just do."

"I trust you," Zane said.

Patience heard Runt pacing behind them. She had a feeling he wanted something to do. From Zane's quivering lips, which revealed his fear despite his attempts to deny it, she decided he did, too.

"Play with Runt. Keep him out of trouble," Patience commanded.

"Yeah!" Zane said. He sounded relieved. She watched as he got into a game of "I'm not touching you" with his baby bronto brother, then turned her attention to G.K.

"I guess we have to talk," she said.

The sailback grunted.

The breeze was facing them, carrying the scents of the three small raptors their way. Patience felt a sudden hunger. G.K.'s stomach rumbled.

"Yeah, I know," Patience said. "It's hard not to go with your instincts."

G.K.'s claws brushed hers. She leaned in close.

"I know why you followed me," she said. "I know why you're here."

She could feel his heart thundering.

"You know I'm trying to go back, and it doesn't make any sense to you. I've got family here. *Real* family. And I've got you."

He nuzzled her. She drew a deep breath and pushed him away.

"I'm sorry," she said. "I can't stay here. This can't be my life."

She looked away. A dozen reasons why she had to go back came to her—

Bertram's warning for one. The future might be changed forever if they didn't stop what might happen here today.

And she missed her world, her life, strange as that might sound.

But there was only one reason that really rang true.

"It doesn't belong to me."

G.K. stepped away from her and hung his heavy head. He looked to the raptors in the distance. They were all blissfully unaware of the existence of the Acros and long-necks nearby.

G.K. roared. He took off in a terrible run toward the trio of raptors that was now looking their way. The ground shook with his footfalls.

Yipping shrilly, the raptors fled.

"No!" Patience screamed. They would go and warn the others. They—

G.K. stopped suddenly, as if he sensed something.

A moment after the raptors cleared the side of the mountain, a thunderous explosion sounded. Patience watched as rock exploded outward, a heavy cloud of dust and debris engulfing the rippling motion of the mountain itself. The ground shuddered. She nearly toppled from her feet.

Then the haze surrounding the area slowly cleared, and forms began to emerge.

The trapped Tenontosaurs!

From the distance, a volley of yips sounded.

Patience looked to G.K., realizing that the young raptors would have been blown apart by the explosion if he hadn't warned them off.

"Great," she whispered, her voice choked with emotion. "You had to make me love you, didn't you?"

The sailback gave no reply.

Patience turned. "Zane, front and center! This is your show now."

CHAPTER 16

WILL

Will was deep inside the mountain when the explosion hit. Rock fell from above, and the walls and floor shook.

"Hook!" he called. "Where are you?"

The wounded raptor didn't answer. Will hadn't expected either Hook or the Microvenator to travel far from the Tenontosaurus cavern. Yet he couldn't find his friend.

His *friend?*

Whoa. Hook was a lot of things to him. A rival. The reason he had been trapped in the mountain in the first place. A crafty, scary predator who had to be watched at all times and made to learn exactly who was boss.

But—a friend?

Then again, Will wasn't really sure what kind of judge he was of true friends anyway. Back at Wetherford, he thought Lance was his best friend, and now he had an idea that things were no longer the way they had been.

Someone tapped him on the shoulder. Will spun, so startled that he nearly dropped his torch. Hook stood before him, silent and a little smug.

Will almost laughed with relief. "How'd you learn to sneak up on me like that?"

Hook simply stared, the fire glittering in his dark eyes.

A voice came from another tunnel. "That's it, Will. How did he *learn?*"

Mr. London emerged from the tunnel. He was alone. "Cari and the guys ran with the other Tenontosaurs. When you didn't show, I figured out what you were doing. I tracked you by scent."

Will bitterly recalled the teacher's coldness toward him. *I didn't know you cared...*

"I thought Albert and Hal and the others were learning," Mr. London said. "And in little ways, maybe they were. But not the way you or I would. Or *him.*"

Will suddenly felt odd about having his back turned to Hook. He took a sharp step away from the raptor—

And saw that Hook was gone.

"Everything I said to you was wrong," Mr. London insisted. "I'm sorry, Will. I really am. This wasn't about you. The machine called to you and Patience and Zane because of things you needed, but it was what I wanted that started it all! It was me."

"Mr. L," Will said. "It's Hook. He's gone. We've gotta find him."

Mr. London kept speaking. "Will, you have to understand. It's crucial. All this was about *me* and what *I* wanted. I wanted to be like you. The hero. The popular guy. And I wanted to have all those years when I had to grow up too fast given back to me.

"The machine gave me that, and I learned from it. That's what Ground Zero is all about. Learning. Evolving."

Will looked around for Hook. Where had he gone? "Mr. L—"

Mr. London took another step closer and raised a hand to cut Will off. "There's a reason why the leader of the raptor pack favored Hook. He's younger than he looks. When he gets older, he's going to get bigger. I had to see him to know that for sure, and now that I have, I'm convinced.

"There are raptors that have been discovered that are a lot bigger than Deinonychus. Hook is the evolutionary link. Ground Zero had nothing to do with saving the Tenontosaurus or the other raptors. It's about *Hook*. If we don't get him out of here before this place goes up, then a link in the chain will be broken. After that, the future as we know it won't happen."

A hiss came from the darkness behind Mr. London.

"Hook," Will said quickly. "He's—"

The little Hypsilophodon was already in motion, darting down another tunnel. Hook ran after him, the splint on his leg shattering and falling away.

Hook wasn't hurt anymore!

He'd *learned* to fake it...

"Nice system you've got here with the markings, Will!" Mr. London called as he was chased by Hook into the darkness.

He pointed at the symbols Will had carved into the wall. "Let's just hope your buddy can't read it!"

Will fought off his surprise and launched himself after Mr. London and Hook. Images of all he had taught Hook raced through his mind. The trick that got him past the Big Guy the first time. The way to patch up a busted leg. And—

"Mr. L!" Will screamed, recalling Hook making some of the markings in the wall himself. "He *can* read 'em!"

Then they were out of sight.

Will heard the roar and crackle of his torch's flames as he tried to follow the tracks they had left. He felt its heat and smelled the burning leaves.

I tracked you by scent, Mr. London had said. He hadn't been carrying a torch. Will had the only torch now.

Yet Mr. L had mentioned the markings. Did he

think Hook was smart enough to know what he had meant by just the words? That he had come to understand some measure of language?

Maybe not, but Mr. L had *pointed* at the symbols. Hook could be going by them *instead* of using his animal instincts.

And that could make him vulnerable.

Will ran down two more tunnels and saw no signs of Hook or the teacher. He stopped and looked at the torch. Something his dad, good old Briefcase Man, used to say came to him:

Sometimes, you just have to go for it.

Will tossed the torch into a nearby cavern. The ground was still rumbling. The tremors Zane and Mr. L had predicted were coming. Debris fell from the ceiling.

Will drew a deep breath and hunted for the same thing Hook was tracking: live prey.

He picked up the scent. It overwhelmed him. As he raced through the tunnels, effortlessly finding his way in total darkness, he felt

HUNGRY-HUNGRY-HUNGRY

His wants, his needs overtook him—they were all that mattered to him. Some part of his brain was registering danger. A scent from the cavern where he had tossed away his torch was gnawing at his consciousness, but he ignored that.

He wanted to hunt. To eat.

To beat his rival to the prey.

All his life, Will had cared so much about what others thought. He'd based his every action on becoming the center of attention and making sure he'd stayed there.

No more.

He felt something so pure, so thrilling, that he didn't know if he could ever go back to being what he was. He had never felt so alive before now!

A sudden change in the scents just ahead made him dive and roll. A sharp wind whipped over his head as a heavy object passed over him.

Will bounded to his feet and heard the object sail inward again. His sickle claws extended—

Click-clack!

He kicked and sliced the hard root in half. Then he withdrew his claws and kicked again, knocking the breath from his attacker.

He didn't need a torch to know who it was: the Microvenator's scent was plain. The root had been one of his discarded torches.

The long-armed predator hopped to its feet and shrieked in rage. The dinosaur raced forward and Will kicked him again, dropping him to the ground.

Tremors wracked the tunnel, and a heavy rock fell from the ceiling. Will leaped out of the way, his senses totally aware of his surroundings, his instincts in full control.

The Microvenator rolled and was only grazed by its fall.

Will scented the air. The prey was close!

He raced from the howling, frustrated predator and soon found himself traveling steadily downward once more. The Microvenator followed, but he was too slow to keep up. Will lost him quickly.

The walls shuddered and more debris fell. This time, a chunk struck Will on the shoulder.

Too much of the roof was falling in for him to avoid it all!

Will saw a dim glow ahead. The ground gave out beneath him, and he tumbled until he was spilled out into the cavern where the Tenontosaurs had once gathered.

A brilliant patch of light burst from a huge gap that had been blown in the far wall.

Then he saw it. The prey! The prey was just ahead, staring at him, waiting, welcoming its end, it was—

FOOD-FOOD-FOOD

"Will!" Mr. London yelled.

It was his science teacher.

Will forced himself to regain control. He realized that he had taken a route he hadn't explored before, one that led him to the tunnel closer to the outside than the one he usually took to reach this place.

Hook flew from that one.

Will looked to the outside. He heard things, saw

things, *scented* things, that were totally impossible.
Yellow taxicabs speeding after Tenontosaurs, forcing them to run in one direction, while speeding

trains and jet cars out of some science fiction movie bore down on the Big Guy and the other raptors, sending them off in the opposite direction.

It was Zane! He was cutting loose, using his imagination and his wild power to separate predator and prey and to give the Tenontosaurus herd a chance to escape!

Will turned to see Hook speeding at Mr. London.

"Run!" Will yelled.

But Mr. London was frozen with fear. Will took two steps to intercept the predator when something deep within the mountain *exploded*.

Debris fell from above, a huge chunk falling on Will, throwing him down and pinning him to the ground.

He watched as Hook raced toward Mr. London, yipping in triumph!

"Hook, please!" Will called.

The predator stopped only inches from his prey. His maw was open, saliva dripping from his sharp teeth, his sickle claw had extended. Hook looked to Will, then to Mr. London. He let out a yip that shocked the teacher out of his paralysis.

Mr. London hesitated only a moment. In the bright sunlight, the teacher pointed at the red body of the raptor in front of him. Will saw Hook's amber markings.

"Amber," murmured Mr. London, as he quickly raced away from the raptor. "Another amber key!"

After allowing the Hypsilophodon to escape, Hook turned and cautiously walked back to Will.

Hook crouched and tried to shove the heavy stone from Will's back, but he couldn't move it. Will felt light-headed. It was hard to think straight.

And he hurt so bad.

Another amber key...another amber key...

Mr. London's words echoed inside Will's pounding skull. Will knew what Mr. London meant. Hook was the evolutionary link, the key to his species' evolution. Hook had to survive or time would be changed—that was the point. That was the most important thing now.

Suddenly, a Microvenator tumbled from a nearby tunnel. He saw Hook, froze in fear, and retreated. Another tremor sealed the tunnel behind him, trapping him.

Will saw debris falling from every direction now. There was no way he was getting out of here.

"Go!" Will yelled to Hook.

The dinosaur hesitated.

"Go!" Will yelled. Only—his scream was coupled with a roar that echoed with incredible force through the cavern.

Will saw a sailback entering the cavern.

It wasn't Patience. The sailback charged at Will—and Hook turned away, running for the water that had kept the Tenontosaurus herd alive for so many days. He hesitated before diving in, looking forlornly at Will the way he might a brother he could not save, then dove in.

G.K. reached down for the chunk of stone that had fallen on Will, and a deafening roar made him freeze.

The light vanished as the cavern collapsed.

Stones fell around Will and G.K., burying them.

Then—for a time—Will knew only darkness.

His breaths were short and shallow. He felt pain rippling throughout his fragile body. The rumbling never stopped, and he braced himself, waiting for the last few rocks to come down, to crush the life out of him—

And a sound that made no sense whatsoever came to him in this darkened, enclosed space. The crackling of lightning. Tendrils of energy passed around and through his body.

Even though there was nowhere to go, Will felt himself rising, passing upward, out of this body and through the stone walls of the mountain. Looking down, he saw a swirling vortex of energy.

At the base of the mountain he saw a Tenontosaurus emerging from a hole that had been created by the explosions.

Tink!

Nearby, he saw a strange collection of dinosaurs standing beside a vast rectangular machine. Patience, Mr. London, Zane, and Runt. The lightning came for all but Runt, and suddenly, Will wasn't alone in the whirlwind.

There were cries. Human cries. Dozens of them.

Below, he saw the Acrocanthosaurus and long-necks eye each other warily as the Hypsilophodon sped away as quickly as he could.

Then—

He was blinking rapidly. A shocking array of scents came to him. Meat loaf. Spaghetti. Milk.

Chocolate milk.

Will sat up quickly and placed his hands in front of his face. His frail, flesh-covered, *human* hands.

He was alive!

Looking around the lunchroom, Will quickly spotted Patience and Zane. He ignored the students who had been gaping down at him and the others.

"Patience! Hey!" Will yelled.

She was slowly coming out of it. The students let him through. He put his hand on her face.

"Are you okay?" he asked.

She looked at him sadly. "I couldn't talk him out of it," she said. "The Green Knight—I tried to make him stay, but..."

She looked away, tears forming at the corners of her eyes. Then she rose and bolted from the lunchroom, her hands covering her face.

Will felt the presence of someone behind him. He turned to face Zane.

"Are you okay?" Zane asked.

For an instant, it struck Will as odd, Zane asking if *he* was all right. But he only nodded.

"Thanks," Will said. "Really. Thank you. It was a good plan. We did it."

Zane offered his hand.

Will took it and squeezed it hard.

"Hey!" Zane said, flinching a little. "I need that."

They walked together through the school, encountering one group after another of students who had been struck by the M.I.N.D. Machine's lightning—and had somehow made it back.

"I don't get it," Will said. "How did they *all* get back?"

Zane shook his head. "Dunno."

At the end of the hall, Will saw Lance. His friend. He and Monique were chatting it up with Leiman.

Lance looked over his shoulder at Will, frowned dismissively, then went back to his conversation with the self-proclaimed leader of the elite.

Percy was there, too, uncomfortably cutting glances between Lance and Will, as if looking for a sign to follow.

Will couldn't help him.

He turned and walked off with Zane. He thought that he had to choose between his pack and a place among the elite—the next logical step in any popular guy's evolution.

But there had been a third choice.

He put his hand on Zane's shoulder and said, "Don't take this wrong, but I really feel like being alone for a while."

Zane grinned. "You know the *funniest* thing? So do I..."

CHAPTER 17

WILL

Will Reilly sat back on the couch and closed his eyes. It felt *so good* to be home. He had a couple of movies from Blockbuster, a bowl of popcorn, and his remote control.

Life didn't get any better than this.

Suddenly, a knock came at the door. Will frowned. Who would be coming around his place tonight?

Will considered ignoring whoever it was, but the knock came again, more insistent this time. With a sigh, he crossed the living room. By the time he had gone through the hall and had his hand on the door-knob, the knocking had evolved into a pounding.

"All right, chill!" Will hollered. He unlocked the door and opened it.

The girl before him was a stunner. She wore a black sleeveless dress. Her hair was piled elegantly high above her soft, delicately defined eyes, cheeks, and lips. The dress clung to her long, lithe form, and her shoes were designer originals.

It wasn't until she spoke that Will knew who it was.

"Am I fashionably late or fashionably early?" Patience asked.

Will controlled his instinctive urge to gape.

He did, on the other hand, feel major league underdressed. His torn jeans, NY Knicks T-shirt, and beat-up sneakers didn't come close to feeling appropriate for standing in the presence of such beauty.

"Early," Will said. "Very fashionably."

"Cool."

She brushed past him and looked around. "Music? Munchies?"

Will shook his head as he led her to the living room.

"Other people?" she asked.

"Not really. I wasn't expecting—"

"They'll be here."

Will watched Patience turn to the music center and pop in a CD.

Whoa. What is going on here?

"I'd get to work on the munchies if I were you," Patience said. "The others will be here soon."

Will just stared at Patience as she elegantly glided across the room. She didn't even *move* like her old self. She seemed so calm. So at peace.

Finally shaking himself back to reality, Will went

to the kitchen and got started on major munchie preparations. After all, he was a party veteran.

He began to hear sounds from the front door. Voices rising above the music. By the time he returned, a dozen people had arrived.

"Great party," some guy Will barely knew announced. Across the room, Patience was ushering Bertram Phillips and Candayce Chambers inside.

It took three trips to bring out all the munchies. By the time he was done, the party's attendees had doubled in number, furniture had been moved, and couples were dancing.

He got Patience on the side. "Gimme a clue."

"Well, you were putting up flyers for a party tonight," Patience said.

Yeah, he thought, *but that was a lifetime ago...*

"But after everything that happened...," Will said. He thought about the school closing, the state agencies coming in, the students who were rushed to the hospital, the press...

"After everything that happened, a party is *exactly* what's needed," Patience said calmly.

Will smiled. "Yeah. I think you're right."

The doorbell rang.

"I'll get it," Patience said excitedly.

Will followed her to the hall. He was expecting to see Monique appear, already picturing the girl's shocked look. Patience had to be doing this to get back at her. Yet something about that explanation just didn't feel right to Will...

The door opened to reveal a thin, red-haired boy in a wheelchair. A pretty young woman, college age, stood behind him.

"Hey, Beanpole," Patience said. Her voice sounded choked with emotion. She looked as if she was struggling not to cry.

Marcus's eyes went wide at the sight of her. "Hey, beautiful!"

Will helped Patience and Marcus's sister get the young man inside. He saw the way Patience was looking at Marcus. Now he understood. She had worn the dress for Marcus, and for the past she was no longer running away from.

Will didn't think he had ever seen anything quite so brave.

"I don't know how long we'll be able to stay," Marcus's sister said to Patience. "The drive was four hours and really took it out of him. But we've got a place to stay and won't be heading back until Sunday, so you two will have plenty of time to get caught up..."

Will faded into the background. He looked at the well-dressed partygoers and felt a strange, sudden urge to steal away to his bedroom upstairs. When he returned, he wore a black suit and a gray T-shirt.

No one looked at him any differently. As Will

studied the faces of the people in the crowd, which had doubled since he'd slipped away, he thought he recognized several students who had been hit by the strange lightning.

There was something in their eyes that marked them. A serenity. A sense of triumph.

He went over to Bertram and Candayce.

"Hey, Ms. Chambers."

"What?" she asked, sounding annoyed. She was practically plastered to Bertram.

"That fund-raiser," Will said. "I thought you might want to talk—"

She silenced him with a single raised eyebrow. "Do I *look* like I'm in fund-raiser mode? Go. Shoo. Dance with your date."

My date? he thought. *I don't have a date.*

Then he looked at Patience once more and smiled. Oh, man. They thought she was his *date!* This was classic. He had to tell her.

She had stepped back from Marcus, who was now surrounded by a collection of students who also hadn't seen him for a very long time.

"Feels good to be back, doesn't it?" Will asked her.

"Feels wonderful."

He stared at her, about to tell her what Candayce had said—when he was overcome by a sudden urge to be close to her. Truly close.

"Let's dance," he said.

She looked away. "Oh, I dunno."

"The world won't end. We've been through *that* already. Come on."

She smiled and took his hands. He led her to a small patch of carpet near the fireplace.

They danced slow, Will holding her close. She held herself stiffly at first, then slowly relaxed.

Will nuzzled her.

Patience drew back, startled. "Why'd you do that?"

His eyes widened. "I—I dunno."

But he *did* know. He had done it because he had wanted to. Because it had felt like the most natural thing in the world to him.

He leaned in close and she let him. He brushed his cheek against hers, and a strange trembling sound came from somewhere deep in his throat.

She shuddered. "G.K. used to do that. How'd you know?"

Will was beyond speaking. Something was happening within him. He felt suddenly as if he were tumbling down into a state that was half-wakeful, half-dreaming.

He stood back from her, raising his jaw, angling it proudly to one side.

Then somehow he knew that he had not returned to the present alone.

"It can't be," Patience whispered.

He had no words. He knew they weren't needed. Instead, he answered her with a sign, a gentle brush of the side of his face against hers, and a look that told her all she needed to know.

"G.K.," she whispered, stunned.

Will had been surprised, too. At first. But he recalled what he had been told, that the Green Knight had sacrificed himself at the exact same moment that Will had given over his life so that Hook might live.

Those selfless acts had linked them somehow, and the M.I.N.D. Machine had snatched the dinosaur's consciousness away just in time.

Its only dilemma was what to do with it. And that hadn't been such a difficult problem, it seemed.

Will was already beginning to like this new inner dino. The strength and love it felt were his, as well.

Patience's eyes registered a quiet acceptance— and a strange excitement.

"So kiss me already," she whispered. "I've been waiting only a hundred million years."

He leaned in close and brushed his lips with hers. The part of him that had once been an Acrocanthosaurus didn't understand this odd custom.

But it felt certain it could grow to like it.

CHAPTER 18

ZANE

Zane stared at the test on his desk. He had marked all the questions and finished the essay.

It had taken him ten minutes.

Taking a deep breath, he collected his books and stood up. Immediately, he felt the stares of his classmates and heard their whispers.

"What's he up to?" someone asked.

"Oh, man, we gotta see this!"

Zane's history teacher, Mr. Klein, eyed him warily. Taking the completed test from his desk, Zane considered that it wasn't too late. He could still turn back.

He waited for some smart remark to come from the Psychic Friends Network about this. But it didn't.

He had considered when he got up this morning that this might not be the best day to try what he had in mind. The school had been closed for nearly a week as investigators attempted to locate the source of the mysterious "electrical fault" that had struck down so many students.

Irate parents had lodged complaints and threatened lawsuits. Some of the "injured" students were still being kept home, even though their physicals had revealed them to be in perfect health.

Everyone was kind of nervous today. Students and teachers alike wondered, was it safe? Or would some other weirdness hit on their first day back?

And here he was, approaching his teacher, test in hand, a full half hour before the bell.

"Bathroom pass?" Mr. Klein asked sadly. He was a portly man in a navy suit, bald on top with a heavy brown beard and mustache.

"Nope." Zane handed him the test.

Mr. Klein looked it over suspiciously. "I see you've filled everything in..."

Zane looked around, trying not to break out in a sweat. He saw the other students watching. They looked anxious and confused.

A guy wearing a bright red baseball cap said, "It's gotta be the essay, it's gotta be!"

"No, he's gonna do somethin'!"

Zane studied his shoes. Everyone was expecting Crazy Zane to pull some kind of stunt.

They were going to be disappointed.

Mr. Klein drew in a deep breath, then let it out again as he read the essay. He gazed at Zane with a vague look of hope.

"You're sure you understand this material?" the teacher asked.

Zane nodded and began to expand on the ideas he had mentioned in his essay. He was speaking for close to a minute before he heard little scratching sounds behind him and realized the other students were taking notes!

"Hey!" Mr. Klein said. "Enough of that!"

The teacher shrugged and handed Zane a hall pass. "Go on, get out of here. You've earned it. I don't know how, but you have."

"Thanks." Zane walked to the door, thinking of all the last-second gags he could still pull. He heard murmurs.

"Zane the brain?"

"No way..."

It would take time for everyone to catch on. And he still wasn't one hundred percent sure he was doing the right thing. But he was tired of doing things for other people. Pulling pranks to entertain them and make them like him. Scoring low on exams because of his fear that he wouldn't be accepted if people thought he had a brain in his head.

It was time for him to start doing things for himself.

He left the classroom without even dropping his pants.

Zane was halfway down the hall when he heard a

scuffle near the stairs. He approached cautiously and saw a bunch of darkly clad truants messing around, shoving each other at the wall.

Zane looked back and spotted the empty desk where the hall monitor should have sat.

Well, it was no biggie. The hall monitor would return from his break soon enough. These guys would move on.

"Yo, Goodyear!" one of the toughs called.

Zane automatically turned to face them.

"Made him look," another one said.

Then they were swarming around him like hungry raptors. Black T-shirts. Leather pants. Boots. Fake tattoos. Strangely colored hair. Pink, purple, and black.

They practically sniffed at him, hoping for a little fear to start their day.

"You got a hall pass?" a guy with a scarlet streak in his hair asked. "We might have to report your fat—"

Zane turned and walked casually in the other direction.

The group followed him out of the stairwell, leaping around him, laughing.

Red came around and blocked his path. "What? Did we upset you? Are you, like, worried we're gonna take your lunch money or something?"

Zane stared at the guy. He thought about how

afraid he had always been in situations like this. And how Will or someone always came to rescue him...

"Yeah, lunch money," another of the hyenas said. "It's not like he couldn't do to lose a few pounds!"

Zane walked ahead, staring right into Red's eyes.

The guy darted back, surprised, a little off-balance. His breath quickened. "Hey, we're not done with you!"

Out of the corner of his eye, Zane saw one of the others dart forward, hand raised to slap the books out of Zane's hand.

Zane moved more quickly, yanking his books out of the way. The other guy's momentum carried him forward, and he fell against a nearby wall.

His "friends" all laughed at him.

Zane shook his head. "I could open any of these doors and have you guys in detention in a second. Or you could walk away. Your choice."

Red gave a nasty little laugh. "You'd go running to teacher. Save me, save me!"

Zane was bigger than Red. A *lot* bigger. He moved in close, until he was practically standing on the other guy's scuffed boots.

"No," Zane said. "To save *you*."

Zane's gaze narrowed. He wasn't the least bit afraid.

Maybe these guys could swarm him and bring him

down. *Maybe*. But it wouldn't happen without a fight.

Red looked away. "Yeah. Right."

But Red turned anyway. And his hyenas followed him as he retreated to the stairs and vanished.

A moment later, Zane heard footsteps. The hall monitor appeared. He was short, with a black crew-cut and big friendly eyes. He wore a flannel shirt and jeans. He looked surprised.

"Hall pass?" the monitor asked.

Zane showed it to him.

"Well, go wherever you want, then. Library, study hall, take a walk. It's up to you."

Zane smiled, realizing for the first time in so very long, it really, really was.

BERTRAM

Bertram had been watching Mr. London all morning. The eighth-grader had skipped two classes and been late to three others, all so that he could unobtrusively keep an eye on the teacher.

Something was going on. Bertram had been unable to reach Mr. London at home after the school had been closed. He had gone to the man's apartment half a dozen times, but Mr. London hadn't come to the door, even though his car was in the parking lot.

He and Mike Peterefsky had come to the school twice in the middle of the night, hoping to get in and dismantle the M.I.N.D. Machine. But insurance investigators and scads of engineers and other technical types were there. They had been working around the clock to make sure the school was safe.

Bertram could have told them where the problem lay. But who would believe him?

There had been no choice but to wait until today.

Bertram and Mike had arrived at school this morning with a backpack filled with tools; only—a lock had been placed on the basement door!

Bertram figured that Mr. London could get the key pretty easily.

But Mr. London had been just as elusive at school as he had been over the weekend and during the early part of the week, when the school was shut down.

Now Bertram stood outside the auditorium leading to fifth period study hall. He had seen Mr. London go in and had waited until the final bell had sounded to make sure the man wasn't coming back out again.

Bertram saw the hall monitor eyeing him, and so he entered the study hall.

The auditorium always reminded Bertram of the stadium seating at the local multiplex. Row after row of chairs angled down to an orchestra pit before a large stage.

Mr. London sat in a chair off to the side. Thirty or so students were scattered around the auditorium, quietly chatting or doing homework. Mr. L was grading papers. He looked up and smiled as Bertram approached.

"I thought you had a class this period," Mr. London said mildly.

"I need to talk to you," Bertram said, pulling up

a seat. "You didn't return my calls."

"I took a flight out Friday to UCLA. Interviewed for a position on Monday."

"Oh," Bertram said.

That explained why Mr. London's car was at his place. He must have taken a cab to the airport.

"They made me an offer before the day was out. I spent until yesterday thinking about it, then turned it down and came back on a late flight last night. I figured I'd see you here today, and that your dad wouldn't appreciate a call at one in the morning."

Bertram nodded. Then he frowned. "You turned it *down?* Why?"

Mr. London looked around with a wide smile. "I like it here. I belong here."

"And..."

The teacher shrugged. "Why does there have to be anything more?"

"We both know why."

Mr. London's smile faded. "I have to go back."

Bertram's face flushed. "No!"

His shout drew the attention of every student in the auditorium. Mr. London sighed and waved them back to their various tasks.

"Bertram, you know I wouldn't even consider activating the machine again if there were any other choice. I learned what I had to learn."

"Then why go *back?* You didn't see what was happening here. People were changing. The entire world was turning into something else."

"I believe you," Mr. London said.

"Then help me get the key to the basement so we can dismantle the machine."

Mr. London looked at the students gathered in the auditorium. He leaned close to Bertram. "See that seventh-grader in the gray sweatshirt? Five rows back, all the way to the left?"

Bertram scanned the rows until he found the guy. The seventh-grader had short-cropped blond hair and wore thick glasses. He glanced furtively at Mr. London, then tensed and looked away quickly.

"His name is Paul Mercer," Mr. London said. "He was one of the twenty-seven students collected by the M.I.N.D. Machine. I bet he has a story to tell."

The teacher rose and walked over to Paul. Bertram followed. They sat in the row in front of the younger guy, who looked at them nervously.

Now that Bertram thought about it, a lot of students had looked at Mr. London strangely today. And all of them had been hit by the energies of the M.I.N.D. Machine.

"Forget what I told you," Mr. London said to the student. "We need to talk about what happened."

Paul went pale. He started to sweat. "I don't—"

"Things have changed," Mr. London said. "It's

all right to tell. Go ahead."

Bertram watched as Paul shrank a little into his seat.

"I shouldn't," Paul said. "You told me not to."

"But I'm telling you it's all right."

Paul leaned forward, clutching his books. "You said you'd say that!"

"I did, didn't I?"

Nodding, Paul drew back again. "I'm sorry. I didn't get it then, and I don't get it now. But I just can't."

Mr. London patted Paul's shoulder. "Good lad."

Bertram followed Mr. London back to his chair near the front of the auditorium.

"What was that supposed to prove?" Bertram asked.

"He was back there," Mr. London said. "Back in the Mesozoic."

Bertram had suspected that the other students had gone back in time. What he couldn't understand was how they had all been brought back when Will, Patience, Zane, and Mr. London had returned.

"I've never spoken with that student before," Mr. London said. "Never. He's never been in one of my classes. I wouldn't even have known his name if I hadn't asked around. But *he* knows *me*. He remembers a conversation we had. One in which I instructed him not to talk about what happened to him in that other time. Do you understand what that means?"

Bertram did. "You think you were back there with him."

"With him and with all the others. I went on a series of rescues."

"But that didn't happen!"

"Not for us. Not *yet*. We both know that time travel is tricky. Their adventures, with me at their side, have already happened for them."

Bertram felt overwhelmed by the possibilities.

"This is why *everyone* came back at once," Mr. London said. "Because I was there to help them find their way. If I decide now to dismantle the machine, then I could just as easily dismantle all of time. The possible reality you saw coming into existence could still arrive."

"There are other explanations," Bertram said desperately. "The M.I.N.D. Machine might have sent you on those rescues before bringing you back with the others, then wiped your memory clean of everything except what happened with Will, Patience, and Zane!"

Mr. London thought about it for a moment.

"Maybe it was some kind of glitch," Bertram added. "And if that's the case, then going back again could threaten reality all over again. We should leave well enough alone and take the machine apart. Like you said you were going to in the *first* place."

Mr. London hung his head. "I know. It's what I promised to do. I understand how I let you down. I understand how you must feel—"

"You don't understand anything," Bertram said angrily. He got up and stalked away from his teacher.

When he was back in the hall, he walked over to the monitor. The student looked at him in awe.

"You built it," he said.

Bertram suddenly realized this was another of the students taken by the M.I.N.D. Machine.

"You changed everything for me," the hall monitor said.

"Me and Mr. London," Bertram said.

The hall monitor was silent, but something flickered in his eyes. Then he shuddered and looked away. "I didn't see you."

Bertram understood that this was the best he could hope for. Unlike Paul in the auditorium, this student wasn't going to say *anything* else about what happened to him in the past.

Bertram knew what he had to do. The backpack loaded with tools was in his locker. He retrieved them, then went up to the basement door and drew a wrench from his backpack. Bringing the wrench high, he gasped.

The padlock he was about to smash had been removed already!

"Mr. London," he whispered.

Shoving the door open, Bertram heard the all-too-familiar crackling of lightning and the rumble of the M.I.N.D. Machine below. A beautiful matrix of blue-white energies spiraled into the air, engulfing the machine and the man who stood at its controls.

Bertram had believed that Mr. London did not have a key to the basement, and that was all that was keeping him from going back and activating the machine. Now he saw that he was wrong.

He ran down the stairs. "Mr. London, don't!"

"I have to," said the shining man. He glowed with the machine's energies. "I know I'm right about this, Bertram. I was waiting because I wanted to tell you what I was going to do. I didn't want you to feel that I'd lied to you again."

Bertram hit the landing at the bottom of the stairs and felt a strange flow of pure force shoving him back.

"I have to do this," Mr. London said. His hands flew across the keyboard, and a golden ladder of energy rose up from the launch chair and reached out for the teacher,

A rip in the fabric of reality began to open.

Bertram felt overwhelmed as he gazed at the brilliant tear. Light poured from it, as bright as the sun! He struggled to push his way forward. He glimpsed a multitude of realities rapidly exchanging places through the rip.

For a second he looked at a futuristic society populated by flying humans. Then it became a medieval battleground with inhuman creatures waging sophisticated warfare. A man and a woman kissed before a sunset, then the sun collapsed and was reborn.

Creation unraveled in the tear—

"I can control it," Mr. London said. His voice resonated with the echoes of men and women and creatures of every description across time. "It all came back to me the moment my hands touched the keys."

Bertram struggled against the forces separating him from Mr. London. He felt strange energies seep inside him. Either the barrier was getting weaker or *he* was getting stronger.

Mr. London shook his head. "I'll do what must be done, then return. I promise you, Bertram, it won't be like before. It won't!"

Bertram was only barely listening. The blue-white lightning and the amber fires were encircling *him* now. He crossed several more feet.

Mr. London looked worried. His hands were moving even faster.

Bertram approached the vaguely human shape of the shining man. He thought he could still see Mr. London's features. There was a look of infinite sadness on his shimmering face.

Then Bertram was plunging into him, moving *through* him. He heard a million screams, and one of the cries of anguish was his own.

He had meant to stop his teacher, but he knew what was really happening. The machine *had* him. It was pulling him apart. Lifting him, tearing him from his physical body.

He was in a whirlwind he had faced in his nightmares countless times. He knew then that he was going *back*.

Then the darkness claimed him.

When Bertram opened his eyes again, he was in another world.

His body was not his own, yet he stood on two feet. He had power and, he sensed, grace.

He also had claws.

Before him stood another dinosaur. A Dilophosaurus with two colorful parallel crests on the top of its head.

A predator.

Bertram tensed and so did the other dinosaur. He raised his claws defensively—

The other dinosaur did the same.

Weird. According to his other senses, particularly his strong sense of smell, there *was* no other dinosaur. Bertram darted to one side, then the other. The dinosaur before him mimicked his movements exactly.

It was a reflection. He was alone.

Whoa.

The last time this had happened to him, he had complained because he'd found himself in the body of a slow-moving, tanklike, spike-backed Anky-losaurus. His buddy Mike had been thrust into the body of a terrifying T. rex.

This time, he was walking on two legs. He was a predator. His rear limbs were made for running. The teeth in his snout were long and slender, while those in his cheeks were blade-shaped.

He had no way to judge how tall he was, though he knew a full-grown Dilophosaurus was usually a good twenty feet long.

Bertram had a sense that he wasn't full grown. This body was young—and very strong.

His body was gray with amber streaks. His crest was violet, yellow, and crimson.

He was lean and mean.

Cool.

But how was he *able* to see such a clear mirror image of himself? There weren't any mirrors in the Mesozoic.

Unless...

"No," Bertram whispered. He stepped back until finally he saw that he had been gazing into a pol-ished clear reflective surface.

Metal.

A panel from the M.I.N.D. Machine.

Bertram stumbled farther back and now he could see the machine in its entirety. Smashed. Scorched.

It sat at an odd angle before him, half buried in the ground.

"Can't be," Bertram said. "No!"

But it was true. Bertram was in the Mesozoic, the age of dinosaurs, in the body of a dinosaur. And he had taken the M.I.N.D. Machine with him.

There was no way back.

CHAPTER 20

WILL

Will Reilly was in the boys' locker room, suiting up for gym class, when he felt the M.I.N.D. Machine flare into life. He saw no telltale flashes of blue-white lightning. Nor had he heard any students crying out and dropping to the ground. Still, his every sense was quivering.

Danger was approaching from every direction.

Over the past few days, Will Reilly had slowly been coming to terms with his new status as something not entirely human.

It hadn't been easy.

He sensed, even before he left the Mesozoic, that his experiences in the age of dinosaurs would change him forever. He simply hadn't expected those changes to be physical.

His sense of smell had been heightened, sharpened. The emotions of all around him were laid bare by the subtle animal scents they produced.

Fear had a distinct and unpleasant odor. On the

other hand, joy was truly sweet.

He could hear the heartbeats of the other students and guess if they were lying or telling the truth by the rhythms of their hearts. And he could run faster, move more stealthily, and leap higher than before.

But he wasn't any stronger. He couldn't break through walls or lift cars or anything cool like that.

He'd spent two full days at the library, reading up on various medical conditions, trying to make sense of what he was experiencing.

He couldn't. Not from what he read in books. The only thing that made sense to him was that his heightened senses were a result of his psychic merging with G.K., or a final and lasting gift from the M.I.N.D. Machine.

Sounds came from the other side of the row of lockers where he sat with three other guys, Marc McHenry, Duane Schultz, and Evan Londo.

They hadn't felt that anything was wrong. They couldn't smell what he smelled. But they would. Soon.

Will pulled on his tank top and quickly tied his shoelaces. He was already wearing his gym shorts.

"You're going to want to get in those lockers," Will said to the three other guys.

Duane, a dark-haired guy with a hairy back, laughed. "Yeah, right."

Will didn't waste time arguing or explaining. They would see for themselves soon enough.

Gripping the top of his open locker door, Will hauled himself up and over the top of the lockers in a single, fluid motion. He landed on the flat gray surface of the lockers like a cat.

A scratching and scraping came from the door.

A dinosaur entered the room.

Will recognized its genus. When he was in the library, he'd also read about dinosaurs. Every kind of dinosaur.

This was a Troodon. A meat-eater. About eight feet long. It had very large eyes, and each side of its lower jaw possessed thirty-five teeth. No other theropod had so many.

The Troodon's hands had slender fingers with a long menacing claw protruding from its inner fingers. It had reddish brown scales, with yellow wavy lines reaching across its back.

He hoped the lockers would be protection enough for the other three. If not, he'd do everything he could to lead it away.

Then the dinosaur walked over to the showers, turned on the water, and stood beneath the steam.

"Skin feels all rough," he muttered, reaching for the soap and freezing when he saw his own claws.

Will leaped from the top of one bank of lockers to another, then dove through the door leading to the gym. He rolled twice and bounded to his feet.

A deafening roar sounded from the other side of the gym. It heralded a chorus of screams.

An Albertosaurus, a relative of the T. rex, stood near the gym's rear exit, attacking the back hoop-stand.

"I never liked this game!" the dinosaur shouted. "Never! Never!"

Dozens of students raced from the towering Albertosaurus.

Will motioned to the double doors leading to one of the school's main corridors. He ran through ahead of them, looking back when he heard a chirping.

Thirty feet up, clinging to a rope, was a Dromiceiomimus. Its long ostrich-like neck quivered.

"I'm no good at this!" the Dromiceiomimus yelped. "Oh, my!"

Will saw a collection of mats below the dinosaur and turned away. He ran through the hall, the other students at his back, and came to a sudden halt as a pair of Pachycephalosaurs crashed through the doors of two opposing classrooms. The Pachys launched themselves at one another with high sharp wails.

Will vaulted over the dome-headed dinosaurs just as their skulls cracked together.

Farther down the hall, bearing to the left, he saw a pair of Nanotyrannus chasing a young, blond, female student. The ceiling splintered directly above them and an Ankylosaurus fell through, pinning the smaller dinosaurs in place.

The screaming girl escaped.

The part of him that was human wanted to know how this could have happened. But the aspect of Will Reilly that ran purely on instinct understood that the M.I.N.D. Machine was gone. He could no longer *feel* it. When it had gone, it had brought something else in its place.

Dinosaurs.

Will knew he had to come up with a plan. There were people in the bodies of those dinosaurs. At least in some. He wasn't so sure about some of those he had seen. Their human personalities could easily have been overwhelmed and submerged.

That would make these animals very, very dangerous.

He had to get out of there and get help. At the far end of the corridor was a ten-foot-long, agile-looking predator. Will thought it was a Syntarsus. Its maw had small, bladelike teeth and its back was ramrod straight, fused in place. A small crimson crest topped its skull.

Will ran right at the dinosaur. At the last second, he dropped, slid, and kicked the legs out from under the dinosaur.

It screeched and squealed, then Will was past it.

He rose and shoved at the door leading to the

outside. It banged on something on the other side and didn't open all the way.

Will took a step outside and felt *nothing* beneath his feet. Looking down, he saw only an empty, swirling, grayish black void. He backed up. The Syntarsus was on its feet again, and didn't try to attack as Will made his way around the dinosaur.

Will heard screaming and saw students flooding into the hallway. But in a nearby classroom, all the students and one dinosaur were gathered near the windows, staring out at the same swirling mass.

Will entered the classroom, glancing at the dinosaur. It was an Elmisaurus. Nine feet long, with long front hands that ended in sickle claws and heavy, strong back feet. Its head reminded Will of a pit bull.

Terribly familiar scents came from behind Will. He turned swiftly and saw a trio of raptors blocking the door.

"That's the one," the closest of the Deinonychus said as he leaped onto a nearby desk and glared at Will. "The only one who can stop it."

Oh, boy, Will thought. He had no idea what these dinosaurs wanted. All he knew was that there were two ways out of this room. The raptors had sealed off one of the exits.

Turning, he grabbed a heavy globe from the teacher's desk and ran screaming for the huge win-

dows. The students parted swiftly, stumbling back in surprise and fear. Will hurled the globe, smashing the window, and leaped through the open space.

He sailed into the void and whatever waited beyond.

To be continued in
BEVERLY HILLS BRONTOSAURUS

HERE'S A SNEAK PEEK AT

DINOVERSE

#5

BEVERLY HILLS BRONTOSAURUS

by Scott Ciencin

All his life J.D. had dreamed of something like this happening to him. He was free of the life into which he'd been born, free to make his own rules, to decide his own future.

He could go where he wanted. Do what he wanted. No one could stop him. And if they were dumb enough to try, then J.D. "Judgment Day" Harms would show them *exactly* how he had earned his name at Wetherford Junior High.

He looked around the lush green valley and laughed. There were other dinosaurs nearby. He could smell them.

And he was *hungry*...

Low roars came from the distance and J.D. followed the sounds. The stomping of his heavy feet made the ground tremble and he felt a little wobbly, but he guessed that was normal. After all, he was still getting the hang of this new body.

He mashed the earth as he went along. He growled and spat. This place was great!

His neck bobbed and his tail swished. That was a little weird. And for some reason, he couldn't quite focus his vision. He saw different images out of each eye. Everything looked flat. Like a TV show.

Whatever. He'd get the hang of things soon enough.

He climbed a small rise and saw a dinosaur lapping water from a huge puddle. The dinosaur was gray with orange splotches and it looked like a T. rex, only bigger, with jaws that reminded J.D. of a pair of scissors.

The dinosaur's head swiveled and muddy water splashed as it rose to fix J.D. with its dark eyes.

J.D. laughed. "Hey, Ugly, what are *you* lookin' at?"

Ugly was looking at *him*. Drool dripped from Ugly's maw. The gray-and-orange dinosaur sprinted up the rise and stopped just before J.D., studying him. Ugly's breath was rank.

J.D.'s heart skipped a beat as Ugly moved in closer. He hadn't expected Ugly to move so fast. Or to be so *big*.

J.D. blinked, trying to make sense out of what he

was seeing. In his time, *he* was the baddest of the bad. The biggest thing out there. The Tyrant King. It only made sense that he was the same in the age of dinosaurs.

Yet Ugly looked at least three times his size!

Ugly leaned in closer and J.D. saw his own reflection in Ugly's dark eyes.

J.D. had a little head with baby teeth. A neck that had to go back a half-dozen feet. A body that was round and tubby. A tail ending in an itsy-bitsy little point.

He was a long-neck. A plant-eater! A lousy leaf-muncher!

A tiny little defenseless one, too!

Sounds came from behind him. Heavy thumps. The earth trembled. J.D. looked back along his long, blubbery flanks and saw two more enormous forms moving in.

He was trapped.

This wasn't fair! *He* was supposed to be the one scaring everyone. Not the other way around!

Ugly opened his maw, raised his tiny front claws, and roared.

J.D. sensed it was a challenge. One this predator might have issued to another of its kind.

All things considered, though, it was really more of a joke.

Ugly was *laughing* at him.

J.D. launched himself at the bigger dinosaur. Ugly yelped in surprise as J.D.'s round hoofs hit him hard in the belly. Suddenly they were tumbling down the other side of the hill, rolling and bouncing. Ugly's head hit a huge shattered tree trunk and he lay on the ground panting as J.D. floundered to a stop before him.

"You want a fight?" J.D. asked, getting up slowly. "You came to the right guy."

J.D. glared at the dazed predator, ignoring the sounds of Ugly's pals moving swiftly down the hill behind him. "Maybe I am a brontosaurus or whatever. Maybe I'm not as big as some of these other dudes. But one thing I've *never* been is defenseless..."

#5
BEVERLY HILLS BRONTOSAURUS

COMING IN SEPTEMBER 2000

#6
DINOSAURS ATE MY HOMEWORK
by Scott Ciencin

"I'M OUT OF EXCUSES AND *WAY* OUT OF TIME!"

My name is Aaron Aimes. I've been sent to the principal's office more times than I can count. And I've had excuses for everything—from getting out of gym to not doing my homework. No one's ever expected much from me. But it's hard to slide by unnoticed when you're ten feet tall and twenty feet long! I've become a Dilophosaurus, and it's up to me to help Bertram Phillips fight J.D. Harms and save the future. This is my first day at Wetherford Junior High and I'm already out of time. <u>Way</u> out!

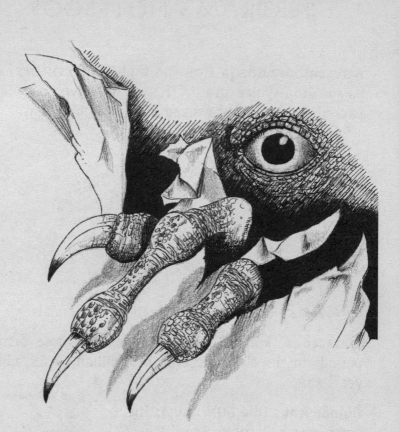

BERTRAM'S
NOTEBOOK

BERTRAM'S NOTEBOOK

Acrocanthosaurus (a-kroh-kan-thoh-SORE-us): The name means "top-spined lizard." It was a 39-foot-long, sail-backed carnivore that walked on its two hind legs.

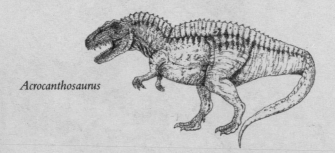

Acrocanthosaurus

Carnivores (KAR-nuh-vorz): Meat-eating animals.

Cretaceous (krih-TAY-shus): The last of three distinct periods in the Mesozoic Era, 145 million to 65 million years ago.

Deinonychus

Deinonychus (die-NON-i-kus): The name means "terrible claw." It was up to 10 feet long and had large fangs, a powerful jaw, muscular legs, and a retractable scythe-like claw on the second toe of each foot. Commonly known as "raptors," Deinonychus were fast and agile and usually hunted in packs to take down large prey.

Herbivores (HUR-bih-vorz): Plant-eating animals.

Hypsilophodon (hip-sih-LOH-foh-don): The name means "high ridge tooth." This dinosaur was a small herbivore, only about four to seven feet in length, but it was very quick. It walked on its two strong back legs.

Hypsilophodon

Iguanodon (ig-WHA-noh-don): The name means "iguana tooth." This was a large herbivore that varied in lengths up to about 30 feet and walked on its hind legs. Its five-fingered "hands" had a spiked thumb, three middle fingers with hooflike nails, and a fifth finger that could be used for grasping.

Iguanodon

Invertebrates (in-VUR-tuh-braytz): Animals without backbones, like jellyfish.

Mesozoic Era (mez-uh-ZOH-ik ER-uh): The age of dinosaurs, 245 million to 65 million years ago.

Microvenator (MYE-kroh-vi-NAY-tor): The name means "tiny hunter." It was a small carnivorous dinosaur that walked on its hind legs and had unusually long arms.

Microvenator

Nodosaurus (no-doh-SORE-us): The name means "node lizard." It was a large armored herbivore that walked on all fours and was related to Ankylosaurus.

Paleontologist (pay-lee-un-TAHL-uh-jist): A scientist who studies the past through fossils.

Pleurocoelus

Pleurocoelus (PLEW-roh-SEEL-us): The name means "hollow side." It was a large herbivore with a long neck and walked on all fours. It is commonly referred to as a "brontosaurus" and is the official state dinosaur of Texas.

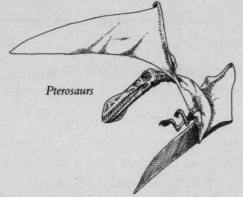

Pterosaurs

Pterosaurs (TER-uh-sorz): Sizable and varied flying reptiles.

Sauroposeidon (SORE-oh-POSI-don): The name means "earthquake-god lizard." It was recently discovered in southeast Oklahoma. Considered the largest dinosaur ever to walk the earth, Sauroposeidon was a long-neck that walked on all four legs, weighed 60 tons, and stood 60 feet tall. It was 100 feet in length.

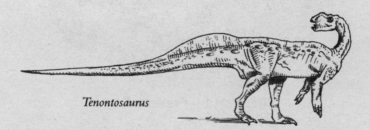

Sauroposeidon

Tenontosaurus

Tenontosaurus (TEH-NON-toh-SORE-us): The name means "sinew lizard." It was a large, horse-faced herbivore with an average length of 24 feet. It could walk on either two or four legs and could achieve great running speed if given time to warm up. In a surprise attack by a predator, however, the Tenontosaurus might lose the chase without time to reach its top speed.

Vertebrates (VUR-tuh-braytz): Animals with backbones, such as fish, mammals, reptiles, and birds.

The World: The continents and the seas of the earth 112 million years ago were different from those in our present day. The inland sea was already through Canada and was starting to enter what would later be the United States. Mexico and parts of many southern states—including Arizona, Texas, Louisiana, Alabama, and Florida—were under water. Parts of Asia were also under water. South America and Africa were still joined together. Australia had broken away from Africa.

The World—Present Day

The World—112 Million Years Ago

SCOTT'S FAVORITE DINO SITES

(and Bertram has them bookmarked, too!)

DINO RUSS'S LAIR
www.isgs.uiuc.edu/dinos/dinos_home.html
A terrific site with lots of dinosaur information, including digs, dinosaur eggs, dino societies, exhibits, books, breaking news, software, and much more.

DINOSAUR ART AND MODELING
www.indyrad.iupui.edu/public/jrafert/dinoart.html
A terrific resource for artists and model-makers interested in dinosaurs. Original art by fans is posted on the site.

DINOSAURIA ON-LINE
www.dinosauria.com
Your window into the Mesozoic! Articles and discussions from enthusiasts and actual paleontologists on various dinosaur topics. Fossil replicas for sale. A dino picture gallery. *The Omnipedia*—a dinosaur encyclopedia at your fingertips, including maps of the ancient earth, dictionaries, pronunciation guides, and more!

THE PALEO RING
www.pitt.edu/~mattf/PaleoRing.html
An ever-evolving assortment of more than two hundred Web sites devoted to dinosaurs and paleontology!

THE PARASAUROLOPHUS HOME PAGE AT THE NEW MEXICO MUSEUM OF NATURAL HISTORY AND SCIENCE
www.nmmnh-abq.mus.nm.us/nmmnh/parasound.html
Very cool—listen to the music of these very special dinosaurs!

THE DINOSAUR INTERPLANETARY GAZETTE
www.dinosaur.org
This site has *everything!* You'll find up-to-date information on the newest and coolest dinosaurs (check out DNN, the Dinosaur News

Network); plenty of links, jokes, quotes, contests, and interviews with authors (like me!) and paleontologists; and much, much more! The *Gazette* is the winner of 22 Really Kewl Awards and is recommended by the National Education Association.

DINOSAUR WORLD
www.dinoworld.net
A "nature preserve" for hundreds of awesome life-size dinosaurs, located in Plant City, Florida, between Tampa and Orlando. I've never seen anything like it! Check it out on the Net, then go see it for yourself!

DINOTOPIA
www.dinotopia.com
I'm the author of four Dinotopia digest novels, *Windchaser, Lost City, Thunder Falls,* and *Sky Dance.* Dinotopia is one of my favorite places to visit. This is the official Web site of James Gurney's epic creation. Enter a world of wonder where humans and dinosaurs peacefully coexist. Ask questions of Bix, post messages to fellow fans, and be sure to let Webmaster Brokehorn know that Scott at DINOVERSE sent you!

PREHISTORIC TIMES
members.aol.com/pretimes
This Web site offers information about the premier magazine for dinosaur enthusiasts around the world—published by DINOVERSE illustrator Mike Fredericks. For dinosaur lovers, aspiring dinosaur artists, and more!

ZOOMDINOSAURS.COM
www.zoomdinosaurs.com
A terrific resource for students. Lots of puzzles, games, information for writing dinosaur reports, classroom activities, an illustrated dinosaur dictionary, frequently asked questions, and fantastic information for dinosaur beginners.

• AUTHOR'S SPECIAL THANKS •

Thanks to Denise Ciencin, M.A., National Certified Counselor, for her many valued and wonderful contributions to this novel. For their assistance in helping me to construct the world of Texas and Oklahoma 112 million years ago, thanks to paleontologists Louis L. Jacobs, Ph.D., Department of Geological Sciences, Southern Methodist University, Dallas, Texas; Professor Richard Cifelli, University of Oklahoma (leader of the team that found the Sauroposeidon); Bonnie Jacobs of Southern Methodist University, Dallas, Texas; and David Nicklin, Chief Geologist, Arco Oil, Plano, Texas.

Thanks to all our friends at the Montgomery School in Chester County, Pennsylvania, especially Daniel and Sandy Mannix, Mrs. Barker's class, Jenna Rebecca Gunderson, and the Hunters; best to Sarah and Caitlin.

Special thanks to Alice Alfonsi, my extraordinary editor, and all our friends at Random House, especially Kate Klimo, Cathy Goldsmith, Kristina Peterson, Craig Virden, Kevin Jones, Andrew Smith, Judith Haut, Daisy Kline, Amy Wells, Mike Wortzman, Kenneth LaFreniere, Artie Bennett, Jenny Golub, and Christopher Shea.

Final thanks to my incredible agent, Jonathan Matson.